The Painter
And Other Stories

Jean Bruce

DEDICATION

This and all other books are dedicated to my family, my friends, everyone who has ever believed in me, and you the reader. Love yourself and the world around you, for love's treasure is that it is versatile, infinite, and everywhere.

CONTENTS

ACKNOWLEDGMENTS

A special thank you to Quills for being amazing friends and an amazing audience, as well as their guidance and advice. Thank you to those that gave me the space I needed to write and to those that asked questions and were engaged with the stories who gave me the courage to continue. You are all amazing people and I am so lucky to know you.

THE PAINTER

The painter was a man who lived alone in a house made for a family. He had two levels, an attic and a basement, four bedrooms, living room, two bathrooms, kitchen and dining room, and they were all filled with canvases and paintings. There was no family; The painter lived with his work. The painter sat with easel and brush in the center of the living room, quiet, immersed, the beast in the image dripping with ink and staining the forest where it stood as it bared its teeth. The painter tapped his brush again into the abysmal color that consumed the beast and, with every stroke, gave it life.

"I see you, beast," the painter cooed to it. His voice echoed through the house to every barren room for each painting to hear. "I see your teeth and claws latching into my skull, tearing your way out, but no need to fuss. I will let you out. You will have your freedom on this canvas. Please be patient."

The painter has not seen a bed in four days. He paints until his life bleeds from him and he has little more strength than to curl up before his current piece, as a dog does to his home, or a dragon to his hoard. His paintings lull him to sleep, then urge him to paint, they beg him to not leave, he stays and he paints. The paintings, his children, consume him. He would spend every second obsessing over his creations without interruption, but with one exception.

There is a knock at the door. The painter gasps and retracts his hand from his beast only to relax and set the tools down. Only two people would bother to visit the painter at his home. One was his manager and friend, who comes to collect some of the more demanded works for galleries and auctions to sell. The other, however, had no need for business. Whatever other reason she had the painter couldn't fathom. He glides to the door, an apparition summoned by the promise of company.

The light invades his home and wrecks his sanctuary. It burns and sears and screams. Among his blinking and muffled cursing, he hears a melody of milk and honey.

"Mr. Rickson, how long has it been since you've eaten? You look like death."

"Forgive me, miss Tempera," a voice of cobwebs and dust responds. "While there is still empty canvas to paint, I seem to care for little else."

"Please Mr. Rickson, do care for yourself. Not only because Mr. Till relies on you in good health but also because I worry about you."

The painter grudgingly accepts the light and is rewarded with her radiant image. Her copper curls flowed from her bonnet, her skin decorated only by garment and lace. Every day she dresses her best. To the painter, she was the gentlest and most modest fair young woman in their quaint little town. Her pink lips rest with a smile, her eyes soft with concern. To the painter, she was the only Angel brilliant enough to warm his sinful, icy existence.

"I'm sorry, miss Tempera. I had no intention to upset you," The painter bowed in apology. "You know how I get about my children."

The woman nodded, "You are so passionate about them, I understand. But I'll not forgive you unless you come have lunch with me. I want to be sure you have at least one proper meal," The woman bent to retrieve a wicker basket and cloth.

"Oh, is it time for lunch already? I'll be a moment," The painter promised before hurrying to his room to attempt a more presentable image. He was not aware of how long he had been wearing the same suit.

"Well perhaps it would be easier to keep track of time if you did not insist on blocking out every window with such heavy curtains," The woman suggested. She braved to peek in, empty canvases strewn about with finished pieces that wait for the manager to be released. Dark, ominous beasts and dead-eyed children peer back at her. 'You are not welcome here,' they seem to say. 'Flee with your accursed sunlight and leave the painter with us.'

"He needs to care for his health," She reminded herself, or perhaps the paintings, with a voice soft as cream. Brave as she may be, she refused to leave her companion, the sunlight. As much as she admired the painter and his passion, she was frightened of his 'children' and the darkness of which they lived.

"How do I look?" The painter asks as he reveals himself.

The woman's heart halts in its tracks. She met with the painter's eyes, glimmering their cool indigo color even in the dimmest of light. She smiled, "You look dashing, Mr. Rickson."

They took solace beneath a large maple tree near a wheat field. The woman unpacked sandwiches and fruit along with other treats.

The painter had forgotten how long it had been since he had eaten until the moment that he saw the strawberries.

"Tell me Mr. Rickson, what piece are you working on currently that has you so immersed?"

"It is a beast," The painter responded. "It comes at night with blaring teeth and thirsty eyes and claws through my heart. I see him when I am in a rage. He has dangerous impulses. I paint him in hopes that it may get rid of some of my own impulses."

The woman's peach face turned downcast. "I understand that your paintings are everything to you, but you do remember what your manager said? Very rarely do your darker works sell, Mr. Rickson. It is why your house is full of them."

"You don't understand, miss Tempera. If I refuse to express these demons that I have within me, they will consume me. My soul is fragile and in pieces, with only paint as my glue and a blank canvas to comfort me."

The woman absently handed the painter a plate. "Surely there is at least… A little more comfort in your life than your paintings."

The painter looked to her. A gleam of golden ray from the sun that he previously scorned formed a halo of light upon the woman's vibrant curls. "I'm afraid I do not understand what you mean," The painter muttered with some understanding, but not brave enough to accuse.

The woman shied away. "Well, you better eat before it all goes to waste. I made you some of your favorites."

"I truly don't know how I can repay you for all that you do for me, miss Tempera," the painter expressed. "You are an angel that I do not deserve."

"Honestly," The woman blushed. "If I did not have any desire for your company, do you suppose I would continue to visit you? Your presence is plenty for me."

The painter felt a moment of panic. It felt as he imagined a bird would feel, falling from its branch before taking flight. In this sudden moment of shock, he took the woman's hand. "I will make something for you. It will be the brightest of masterpieces, a child just for you."

"You know how much I adore you. As an artist, certainly. I am not so sure, however, if I can accept such a gift." His hand, meant to support himself, pulled her to drop with him. She is reminded once more of the paintings taking refuge in the painter's home.

"Just wait, miss Tempera. This painting will hold the part of my soul that you have made good and sweet."

The woman took his hand into both of hers. "Mr. Rickson, I must be honest with you. How I feel…"

"I know," The painter informed her with a nod of his head. "Thank you for the picnic. I must hurry now before the inspiration leaves me, and it becomes dark again." The painter stood and fled back to his home.

"Wait," The woman implored, but he was already too far for her small voice to carry to him. The woman was left there with a mixture of joy and terror. The man she loved made inspiring portraits of soldiers, knights, royalty and poor. He paints about everyday life and playing children. His paintings always sold at a high price, and many times people claim that his art seems to have life in them. His portraits breathed. On the other hand, there were also beasts and demons and shadows. They also seemed to breathe. They seemed to live. With the painter, it was difficult to know what he would stroke life into next. She admired him, and feared him for that trait. One thing was certain, if she left him to work alone for too long, he would starve in that room.

The painter broke the silence with the slamming of his door. He broke the darkness with a pull of the curtains. He left the beast to slumber in the corner of darkness and gave his easel a new opportunity. It had been over a week since he used his brighter colors. His mind still carried the sight of the fair woman. Of all the faults the painter could attribute with the sun, the one point of redemption was the chance to see her again. He sketched and measured while his heart beat loudly, almost painfully. His soul sang with the vision of her.

The night fell, but though the sun no longer remained, the white moon and the stars sang their sweet lullaby and sent their brilliance through the windowpanes, urging him on. He didn't sleep. His heart beat too fast to allow him to. The sunrise emerged and welcomed the vision of the painter's brightest hope. With all the emotions that the painter had given form to, his happiness and sadness, his anger and forgiveness, this was the best of them all. It was a piece of love, a feeling to the painter like being turned to gold with the touch of the fair woman's hand. Her oceanic gaze turned him to stone.

A knock came at the door. The painter, afraid to ruin the

surprise, covered the piece with a white cloth, closed the curtains and went to answer the door.

His manager stood before him. "Have you any new pieces for me?" He asked.

"Mr. Till, I would have a piece ready for you but I have grown madly in love," The painter proclaimed, inviting the manager into his home.

"That is the only way you know how to feel Mr. Rickson. Madly," The manager responded. "Still, though it is unlike you to not have works ready for me by now, I am pleased to know you have something else to occupy your time. Sir, you look a fright. When was the last time you had proper sleep and shower?"

"My apologies, Mr. Till."

"Need I remind you there is an auction tomorrow that you must make an appearance for? I expect you to be properly clean and rested by then, unless you'll never hear the end of it."

"Yes, of course. But Mr. Till, let me sing to you the song in my heart that fair miss Tempera has left me." The painter went to the covered work and presented it to his friend.

Even in its bare skeleton, it revealed itself modestly and reflected in the window light like the face of the moons. "Why, Mr. Rickson. This has to be your most beautiful piece of work I have ever seen. It will be your most priceless piece-"

"It will not be for sale."

The manager turned his eyes to the painter. "What do you mean?"

"This piece is reserved for miss Tempera, for her support and her love."

The manager put a hand to his chin. "I hope you will at least strive to make other pieces like this. They would make us well-off for the rest of our days, I'm sure."

"More paintings of love," The painter murmured. "Perhaps I may. The feeling is certainly in no short supply."

"Truth be told," The manager looked around. "It would be a relief to see less of..." The eyes of the work surrounding them gave the manager a chill down his body.

Once the manager left, the painter continued working on his newest child. The entire day went by, and like all pieces, the painter took the greatest care into every detail. As the night fell, he was reminded of tomorrow. Despite his desire to keep working, he covered the piece and went up to his bed for the first time in a while. He rested soundly, thinking of the woman and her fair skin, her peach lips, and her delicate lace.

He went to the auction, and she was there in the crowd as his paintings were sold one by one. By request, there were two of the painter's darker creations up for auction, but though they were sold, they were the cheapest pieces taken.

"Miss Tempera, might I escort you home today?" The painter asked once the auction had ended.

"Mr. Rickson, why, yes, I would like nothing more." The woman smiled and shyly took his arm. He led her to his buggy and took her straight to her farmhouse where her father waited.

"Thank you for taking me home, Mr. Rickson." The woman gave him a shy smile.

"Not at all, you don't live far from me, and I am more than happy to spend my spare time in your presence. As for your work of art, it will be done in a few days."

The woman turned to him. "Please don't tire yourself too much on my behalf."

"It's no trouble at all, miss Tempera. To be quite frank, I feel as though I'm gliding through the air when I work on your piece. And I must apologize for looking to you during the entire auction. I only want to commit your vision to my memory so I never forget a single detail about you."

The woman's cheeks became a tone redder. "Oh, Mr. Rickson. You will see me tomorrow, and for many days to come."

"Well," The painter concluded. "Then, until tomorrow."

"Yes. Tomorrow."

The painter looked on to the woman's father. His gaze disappointing, judgmental. The painter attempted a smile, but her father only scowled and led his daughter inside. That look irked him. He felt the Beast within him stir beneath the bed of flowers the woman had left there.

He got home to the darkness. The silence greeted him with images of dead-eyed children and creatures from the shadows. He looked to the curtains and then he looked to the easel. He felt the beast growl impatiently within him, but his heart sang with desire to the sight on the woman's face when she saw the child that he made for her. 'He believes you are unfit for his daughter,' the painter heard the Beast say. 'He believes you are a loon.'

"I am no loon. I am an artist. I'll show him that I am fit for his daughter." He set the veiled piece gently down against the curtain and put the Beast back onto the easel. The Beast, with its sharp teeth and long claws, could tear men apart. It would destroy anyone who thought of him as a loon. In the darkness, the Beast growls and bares its teeth. It hunches and howls. It destroys anything it doesn't like. The painter feels his smile twist wider.

Late that night, with the Beast finished, he retired upstairs in his room. He dreamed of the Beast, hunched and baring its teeth at the painter's bedside. He watched the Beast turn and flee. He heard his door open and close, and then silence.

When the painter woke, he felt elated. His mind was clear and his heart was light. "Today I will paint for miss Tempera." he hurried downstairs in his nightgown and to his living room. He saw the Beast on the easel, and red paint spattered randomly along the floor from his room to the front door. None of the paintings were damaged, but the painter thought he had set the Beast down from the easel. Not thinking much from it, he set the Beast down and unveiled his current masterpiece.

He worked from daybreak to dawn, and though he continued to paint while his heart soared with the thought of the woman, she never came to visit as she had promised. As soon as it became too dark to see with the sky alone, he put on some clothes and a light coat and walked towards the farm where the woman lived.

Immediately, the painter noticed things were amiss. Part of the fence around the house was broken, and a lantern was lit in a single room. The door had been broken apart, and inside he could hear crying. "Miss Tempera?" He called out before hurrying inside the home for anyone he could find, rushing into a room where he saw the woman crying and packing up her things. She gasped and twirled to see the painter standing before her.

"Oh, Mr. Rickson!" The woman cried before rushing into his arms. Her shoulders shook and tried as she may to calm herself, she felt hysterical. "This creature, it came last night, it took my father away, there were claws and teeth and I could only hide. My father is gone, Mr. Rickson, I'm to live with my aunt by the bay side."

"The bay side," The painter mused. "But that's so far away."

"I'll be returning for my father's funeral this Sunday. Mr. Rickson, I'm terrified of this house, I don't know what else to do.

I've been sick thinking of my father, I can't stop crying. I can't stay here. No one can find what took my father, it may still be out there."

"That is concerning," The Painter hugged her tight before grabbing her shoulders and looking into her large green eyes. "If we must part for your safety, then I will think of you every day. When you arrive on Sunday, I will have my piece for you to remember me by. Please do not forget me."

"I could never forget you, dear Mr. Rickson. The creature was seen heading towards your house, please be careful. I am mostly worried about you," She admitted, resting her head on his chest.

The painter saw her to the station to leave him for a few days. His heart was heavy with her loss, but also filled with dread at the thought of her being in danger. When he arrived home, he looked to the paint splattered on the ground. He had a strange desire to clean his living room. He put all his works into the closet and the empty canvases against the walls. He swept and mopped and brushed away the cobwebs. He remembered how, when they were still acquaintances, the woman urged the painter to clean away the dust so as to keep his art healthy. He couldn't keep up with the cleaning, but on the days he did it always made him feel better and reminded him of how she cared for him since the beginning. She was a scholar, known well for her knowledge and care for stories and art. She never liked the farm, she preferred to live in the city. The bay side was a large city, perhaps she would be happy there.

Looking to his current masterpiece, he thought of her. He painted, thinking how scared she must be. He thought of how lonely she must feel tonight on that cold train. Perhaps he should have gone with her, but that would be improper considering the circumstances. He thought of whatever creature could have taken the farmer. He imagined a wolf or bear, then thought of how if he were there, he would have protected the woman to his dying breath. This painting would be filled with love and protection. "With this work of art, miss Tempera will never feel pain or loss ever again. I wish I was there to protect her. It breaks my heart to see her in tears." The painter took a step back to view his painting. No, it wasn't good enough. For her, it had to be his best work.

Five days passed until Sunday arrived. The Painter finished his masterpiece, and he looked to it with a sense of pride and excitement. He dressed his best and, with masterpiece packaged and handled, he hurried to the funeral where he would see his truest love.

As he arrived, he searched for her from every buggy and every carriage. She didn't arrive until near the end, her face veiled to hide her tears and her lace as dark as death. He walked up to her as she was being escorted by her brother who had moved away some years before. Although her brother didn't seem pleased to see the painter, the woman pulled her veil back with a look of surprise. When he saw her face, his heart leaped. Her face was tired. What was rosy and peach was now white as porcelain. Her smile seemed old, as though she almost forgot how to twist her lips upward. The painter took her hand.

"I know I was no friend of your fathers, and it may not be proper for me to be here. However, I just came down here to give you this." He handed her the wrapped-up work of art. "I call it, 'Fairest Lady Tempera.' It's in honor of you and all that you have done for me."

"Mr. Rickson," The woman breathed. "This is such a wonderful surprise, thank you."

"I told you I'd have it done," He reminded her.

"Yes, but," She started. "Forgive me if I sound silly, but I had thought in your passion and your art, you would have forgotten about me while I was away."

"Miss Tempera," The painter proclaimed. "Even if I live to be a hundred years old, and every day is filled with nothing but art and solitude, I would never even for a day forget your radiant smile or your warmest heart."

"Oh, Mr. Rickson," The woman breathed. Her brother cleared his throat, and once more she was brought back to reality. "Please keep this with you for now, but stay for the service. I want to come with you to your home and speak with you before I leave again. Then I will see it."

"As you wish," The painter replied. He allowed the woman's brother to take her closer to the service. She put the veil over her face. The painter felt out of place at the service, but he held the wrapped painting close to him. It was a source of comfort, and he hoped it would be for the woman as well.

The woman's brother felt disdain towards the painter, but for the sake of his sister, he took her to see him. The brother waited in the buggy as she met him at his doorstep after the service. The painter handed her the child he made for her.

"Please open it now. I want to see your reaction," He urged.

She took gentle care in opening the package. As the paper fell away and the picture was exposed for the world to see, the woman gasped and covered her mouth. Tears welled up in her eyes as she witnessed the image before her.

Fairest Lady Tempera was an angel in a halo of light. Her soft, copper curls touched with gold. Her body was dressed in soft, delicate white lace adorned with equally delicate white wings. She sat, emerald eyes cast down as she sat on a silver bench, one hand holding open a book and the other on a young man's head that rests at her lap. Brushes and paint lay on the ground beneath them, the man in black and the fair angel providing comfort on a park bench near a hill with a large maple where the painter and the woman often had their picnics. It was, to the woman's delight, a perfect time capsule of the great moments they had together.

"This is the most perfect piece I have ever seen, Mr. Rickson. I'm not sure what to say."

"I know what I wish to say, miss Tempera," The painter took a hand in hers. "I love you. From the bottom of my heart."

"Mr. Rickson," The woman wept. "For so long I've wanted to tell you how I felt, but now I don't know how to say this."

The painter noticed the quarrel in her eyes. He felt his racing heart slur. "What's the matter?"

"Mr. Rickson, since my father's death, my aunt and brother has started to talk about marrying me off. They say it'll be what's best for me, I've tried to protest, but you know how... Angry my brother gets."

The painter turned his eyes to her brother's buggy. "He doesn't hurt you, does he?"

"Oh, nothing like that," She assured him. "But he gets loud and he won't listen to me. He knows that I, well, I've always wanted you to court me. But my brother doesn't think you'll be a good man for me."

"Why is that?"

"He just doesn't think a painter can support a wife and children."

The painter clenched his teeth. "I have the land my parents left me, I have a steady career, I could make more money if I wanted to. I am twice the man that anyone can boast."

"I know that," The woman smiled. "But my brother is the last man in my family. I have to respect his wishes."

"You shouldn't have to worry about anyone's wishes but your own," The painter growled. "You are brilliant enough to make your own decisions." He gave her a pleading look, "Elope with me."

"I can't," She whimpered. "I do not want to lose any more of my family, my heart couldn't take it." She pulled the ribbon of her bonnet and handed it to him. "I will keep trying to persuade him to reconsider. I'll ask if there's anything you could do. I'll come back for you."

The painter took the bonnet. "Keep the picture, and me, close to your heart. I love you."

"I know," she smiled. "And I will. I love you, too. We're leaving for the train first thing tomorrow. I'll write you every day."

The woman hurried to the buggy, canvas in hand. She waved to the painter and he waved back. The brother glared. The painter clenched his teeth.

That night, the painter went to sleep with the bonnet on his nightstand. He had another dream of the Beast. It growled and writhed. Her brother didn't think he was worthy of her? Her brother hasn't even been around for the last few years, how could he know what was best for her? If the brother was out of the way, then nothing would be standing between him and his fair lady. If the brother were dead, then it wouldn't matter what he thinks about the painter. If he were dead...

"Miss Tempera would be so distraught," He whispered to the Beast. "I do not want to see her in tears anymore. I want her to be safe and happy."

The Beast bowed his head and bounded down the stairs.

When morning came, the painter awoke to an abrupt rapping on his front door. He sat up in bed, waited a moment, then once the rapping returned, he stumbled his way downstairs.

"Mr. Rickson!" The woman exclaimed as she wrapped her arms around his neck. "I was so worried, I'm glad you're alright!"

The painter blinked, yet responded to the hug regardless. "Of course I'm alright, miss Tempera."

"Then why did you leave so suddenly? After that creature attacked you, I thought you were in serious pain."

"Creature?" The painter mused. "Miss Tempera, I'm afraid I don't know what you're talking about."

"Last night," The woman continued. "The creature was after my brother and you saved us from it. You came out of nowhere, then once the creature turned and left you disappeared without a word! My brother was in so much shock that I had to take him to see a nurse late last night but I came as soon as I could to see you and to thank you. My brother thanks you, as well."

The painter, confused and unsure of what to say, could only nod and reply to her luminescent smile, "Anything for you, miss Tempera."

"And you will be proud of me," The woman grinned. "When my brother was being treated, I sang your praises. I told him that if you were there to save us then you would have the ability to protect me for the rest of our lives. I told him that you were so brave to turn away the beast. He was still hesitant, but then he asked me if you made me happy."

The painter kept his gaze to her, his heart beginning to race. "What did you tell him?"

"You should know by now how I feel, Mr. Rickson. I said, 'Yes, more than anything.' I told him that, if you would ask for my hand, I would not hesitate."

"Then," The painter held her hands in his. "I will not hesitate either. Let's go to your brother immediately, I'll ask for his blessing. I will marry you before this year ends!"

The painter raced with the woman to the farm where her brother lay bedridden. The house, previously mended and further reinforced, had been torn down once more by the monstrous creature. The painter came before the brother. "Mr. Tempera, I apologize for last night."

"You have no need to apologize. If it weren't for you, then I wouldn't even be here. I should be thanking you."

The painter felt unworthy of praise, but if it led him closer to having the woman he loved, then he would become the hero of the day. He only hoped the true hero, whoever he was, wouldn't reveal himself anytime soon. "Mr. Tempera, I do not mean to ask this of you while you are healing, but I cannot hold myself back any longer. I wish to marry miss Tempera, and guard her with my life. I ask for your blessing."

The seconds of silence that followed stabbed into the painter's heart with such force that he feared falling over. The brother studied the painter's face as though the painter might be abstract or slowly fading away.

"Be good to my sister," The brother demanded. "I warn you not to let a single day pass where she feels helpless."

The woman cried out in joy, wrapping her arms around her bedridden sibling. The painter felt his chest rise. He felt as though he could crow with the rooster and fly with the pheasants. He chained his enthusiasm as tightly as he could and bent his waist towards the brother. "You have my word that I will make miss Tempera the happiest woman alive."

They had wed in the early fall. The painter and his bride arrived to a home they now shared among the empty canvases and dark paintings. The paintings were moved to the basement because they unnerved the bride, the only exception being 'Fairest Lady Tempera,' which hung in the master bedroom. The brilliant painting stood proud, the angel with the copper curls sitting in the presence of the painter, his head resting on her lap, a sleeve on his black suit lightly torn.

TRINKET

A homeless soul trapped in an object, I sit and wait. I do not move. I move slightly. I sleep until I'm stirred. I can be vengeful, loud and animate. I can be timid, slow and benign. I used to be like you. I used to have a life and feelings. I used to have dreams and wishes. Now I sit here, lost and scared. Cursed and hateful. There are more of us. We are everywhere, and can be anything. We are clocks. We are portraits. We are books.

Help us.

We were first a soul that met an unfortunate end. Sometimes, our end was from the very object we possess. We are doomed to repeat our fate, but some are luckier. Sometimes we are able to move and send messages. Other times, we are only strong enough to respond with a single jump, or action. Even so, we are all trapped in the same way.

Free us.

We do not know how we got trapped. We do not know how to escape. Sometimes it's a ritual. Sometimes it's destruction. Sometimes it's love. If done the wrong way, it will warp us. Twist us. Make us monsters. Make us evil. Save us.

Sometimes we are too far gone. Sometimes we enjoy the power. Sometimes we enjoy the company. We've found home in our cages. We may not know. We may know and not care. We may care and not wish to be trouble. We are dolls. We are jewelry. We are vehicles. We are trinkets.

Stop us.

PRINCETON'S JOURNAL: TIMOTHY

Hello brother, it's Princeton. This job's study has been very interesting. It might have some information on how a demon relates to humans, but I'll leave it to you to decipher this investigation.

I was recently hired to eliminate activity in this small building located at a rural mountainside. I drove up and didn't arrive until late at night. Sandra fell asleep a couple hours before arriving. She was so excited to come that she exhausted herself. The couple that lived in the house mentioned that they were always stressed and their relationship had become toxic, as though something was sucking their joy away. The husband felt unsure about the idea of demons, but the wife was completely certain. I have to admit, from the moment I entered the yard I felt uneasy. Sandra came with me to the room we were meant to stay. The couple left for a weekend to try and enjoy a deeply needed holiday. Sandra wanted to look around the whole house, but I convinced her to come with me to the bedroom and go to sleep. I promised her we'd start looking around once the sun rose.

There was a rooster nearby that would not stop crowing that morning. I hardly slept that night. I kept thinking that I heard noises and whispers in the house. There was certainly something there, but since it was daylight, Sandra and I were in less danger to investigate. I made Sandra breakfast and started looking through the first floor. Sandra didn't even finish her breakfast before she rushed upstairs when my back was turned.

The house was a mess, no wonder the place felt depressing. Full garbage bags were tossed to the side. The counter was covered in dishes, there were boxes full of dusty things and expired food items. "It's like no one's cleaned this place in years," I mused.

I was reminded of the old tale our grandma used to tell us of how moving furniture and cleaning would ward off spirits. Perhaps there is some truth to that tale.

"Dad," I heard Sandra cry. I hurried upstairs to see there were only two rooms in the second floor. One was a bedroom with no furniture in it, the other was a bathroom that was dusty and unused. Did the couple not even use this second floor? Sandra was in the room, looking towards the walk-in closet. I came up to her and carefully opened the closet.

"Sandra, stay back," I warned her. I thought I saw something just at the corner of the closet. It looked like a white mask. It was gone when I peered closer. Sandra looked up at me. "He's sad, daddy."

It's a good thing that I can take her on some of these trips. She has a gift for understanding these beings better than most. Considering the danger, however, I sometimes wish my allergies wouldn't prohibit me from having a pet. They're supposedly just as good at sensing spirits and demons as children. It would also be interesting to test that rumor, but I digress.

"Well we shouldn't bother him right now," I picked her up. It was at that point I lamented how light she was for an eight-year-old. It's hard enough to feed her with her allergy to gluten, but she also has to be so difficult when trying to get her to eat. I took her downstairs to finish her breakfast and headed to the basement.

It was more crowded in the basement than inside the house. I couldn't make it farther than the door. I saw tunnel webs and molded-over spiders. Everything had such a thick layer of dust that I couldn't make out anything. Out the corner of my eye, I thought I saw something wrapped in bandages move. I looked over, but there was nothing there except more webs.

"Sandra, you better be eating your breakfast up there!" I called up. She didn't respond. I walked up the stairs and sure enough, she wasn't sitting at the table. "Sandra," I sighed.

I walked back upstairs and, as I had suspected, she was holding out her hand towards the closet. "Come on out," She whispered. "I won't hurt you."

"Sandra," My call startled her and she put her hand behind her back. "Sweetie, leave him alone for now. It's daylight; the rooster's still going at it. It's too loud and bright for them to be wandering around. Let him stay there until it gets dark." I was afraid she may have been angering whatever was inside the closet.

She looked over to me, but didn't move from her spot.

I took off my glasses and rubbed my eyes, taking a moment to calm myself. Sandra kept her big gray eyes on me, hands behind her back. I knelt down to her level. "You know how it feels for you sometimes with being touched," I told her. "Well, with daylight, it's the same for most spirits. They get overwhelmed and lash out. Loud noises and bright lights hurt them. Do you understand?"

Sandra nodded, but still she didn't budge.

I let out a deep sigh and put my glasses back on. "Okay. How about if you go down and finish all your breakfast, you can come up and keep him company, but don't try to make him come outside. We'll wait until dark before we try to do that. How does that sound?"

That deal seemed to satisfy her. Sandra passed me to go downstairs and eat. I took this opportunity, while I was alone, to whisper to the spirit. "She means you well."

Even knowing they're around, it still feels silly to speak out loud to them. I remember you mentioning that it helps, at the very least, to calm my nerves. Even so, there is always that fear that I may be talking to myself. It's still strange at times to admit that I get paid to talk out loud to imaginary friends and wander around abandoned places. To the eyes of a skeptic, I'm a man who travels at the request of paranoid landowners to wander around, say whatever will make the landowner happy, then do some phony ritual to make the landowner pay me. In this case, the ritual might be to clean the house.

It seemed to me like the demon was hiding in the only place not cluttered with stuff. Perhaps the claustrophobia was causing unrest. It wouldn't be the first time. Paranoid people attract paranoid demons, that much we've proven. Still, I was sure that there was something more about this household. Whatever I saw in the basement for a second, if it wasn't a trick of the eye, must have also had some connection with the couple. It was too soon to tell, however, if there were any demons at all. I had to wait until it got dark.

I thought about the couple for a while as I stood alone in the empty room. It was hard to determine whether it was the haunted house that caused their hostility, or their hostility that haunted the house. If this wasn't error due to an overactive imagination, there was a passive demon in the upstairs closet and something in the basement. If Sandra was correct about the one in the closet, then his hiding and lack of activity towards the rest of the house assured me it was a passive demon. If I was right about the demon in the basement, it was still too soon to tell if it were the culprit for the hostility.

It was a bit strange for Sandra to be so interested in a passive demon, though. Passive demons and spirits are hard to detect and do almost nothing to anyone. They just hide and do their routine until, we guess, they fade away. The active or hostile ones are usually the ones Sandra can't help but antagonize. Poltergeists, trinkets, and summoned demons are normally what Sandra walks up to and it nearly gives me a heart attack. I could only wonder what caught Sandra's attention so much about this passive demon in particular. I doubted Sandra would be able to explain it herself.

I got downstairs to see Sandra having trouble eating breakfast, but at least this time she was eating. I often wonder if she'd be better off spending her summers with you, but if she did that, I'd never see her. We both love Sandra, but I never stop wondering whether I'm a proper guardian for her. You have a stable house with a huge library and neighbors with children for her to play with. I have difficulty with even just getting her to eat half the time. I tried to shove the thoughts away, there was still work to do.

After breakfast, Sandra sat in a corner of the empty room watching the closet. I went up every so often to check on her as I got some supplies out of the car for when it got dark. I brought up her lunch and dinner and we ate in the room upstairs. She had an easier time eating lunch, but I ended up having to put away the rest of dinner for leftovers. "It is awfully curious how this room is the only one with nothing in it," I wondered aloud. "It's so cluttered everywhere else," And I was honestly starting to feel a little restricted.

"I don't think he likes the clutter," Sandra replied. "This is the only place where he feels safe."

I was startled at her response. I wasn't really expecting a response, nor did I think Sandra would know the answer to the question I kept asking myself. Was this demon speaking to Sandra somehow? "Safe from what?" I asked her. "Do you know?"

Sandra shrugged. "Them," she responded.

With the sky growing darker, and the moons above greeted the first stars, I noticed Sandra offer her hand towards the closet. It was easier for me to see him in the darkness from the corner of my eye. The figure kept shifting with the shadows, but the one constant feature was the white mask, cracked and nearly shattered on his face. The expression was sad. It reminded me of the 'tragedy' mask seen in dramas.

I have caught glimpses of dark ethereal humanoid beings before, but this was the first time I ever saw one wearing a mask.

He poked out a little, his movements static and jagged. He tilted his head towards Sandra, then looked towards the entrance of the room and retreated again in the closet.

"Curious," I mumbled. I looked down to Sandra. "Sandra wait here okay?"

Sandra looked up at me and nodded.

The demon in the closet was afraid of something. I wondered if it could have been the demon in the basement. Sandra said he was afraid of 'them,' so I thought there must be a more violent being haunting the house after all.

I left the room, keeping on as little light as possible, which made going through the house difficult with all the clutter. I almost tripped down the last couple stairs. Once I made it to the bottom, my eyes caught something that stood out in the moonlight. It looked like a body, black strands of hair protruding out of the bandages. Fear got the better of me, and I turned on the light.

There was nothing there.

It took a moment for me to catch my breath. Once my bearings were gathered, I started to rummage through the boxes for clues. It took me nearly an hour, but I came across a box of books about chi and other spiritually related topics. "These are probably books belonging to the wife," I muttered. She seemed much more open to spiritual influences and she was the one who called me here. Among these series of books, I encountered one about Demonology.

"Hmm," I wasn't impressed. There was merit to these books to some degree but they were pretty determined to discredit any indication of demons that weren't the scary ones. Fear was the biggest moneymaker, and it did more to scare people than to educate them.

I saw the bandaged figure out the corner of my eye.

I didn't look its way this time. "Didn't I see you in the basement before?" It didn't move.

While the bandaged figure was around, my body felt tense and my breathing went hollow. I felt crowded, like I was the one wrapped in bandages. I tried to ignore the feeling and closed the book on Demonology, looking down to find more books. My eyes landed on a book describing exorcisms. My eyes widened, and I thumbed through the book.

"I think I'm beginning to see the connections. The demon

upstairs is afraid of you, isn't it?" I looked around and could find no sign of the bandaged figure, but I still felt tangled. Did the wife attempt to exorcise the bandaged figure and succeeded only in making it angry? It was possible that the demon hiding in the closet was one that brought forth comfort and safety. It was possible that this apparent demon of clutter overtook the home and dominated it as the wife and husband got messier, pushing the demon of comfort into the closet and making the relationship with the couple worse over time.

I stopped at an illustration that I caught while thumbing through. "wait," I muttered. "This isn't what I expected." The images weren't depicted as masks, but there were white faces. These ghostly, white faces with plastered expressions of horror, anger and desperation. One of the faces looked much like the mask the one upstairs wore.

"So, it was an exorcism," I sighed. But it wasn't a failed one. This was an exorcism that was forceful, violent, and sloppily done, but successful. These forceful approaches really did more harm than good. The two demons had less to do with each other than I thought.

The bandaged creature loomed right behind me. I couldn't see it, but I could feel it. The demon upstairs, I realized, wasn't passive at all. It was a personal demon, one that lived in the wife's heart. She exorcised him, and when she did, she opened the door for a new demon to arrive. The bandaged demon had nothing to do with the closet demon, it only saw an opportunity to feed off of the unrest that was left behind. The demon in the closet wasn't afraid of 'them' as in the bandaged creature, he was afraid of 'them' as in the husband and wife. I closed the book and went back upstairs. As I headed up the stairwell, I heard Sandra talking. "Daddy isn't like that," She said. "We help demons."

"Sweetheart," I walked through the door and jumped when I thought I saw a blur of something rush towards the closet. Sandra looked up at me in surprise.

Sandra sighed audibly and her body slumped. "You scared Timothy."

"Timothy?" I parroted. "Is that what he says his name is?"
Sandra nodded.

I asked her to tell me what else he told her. As I found out before, he used to be a personal demon. The wife of the house fantasized of a perfect man to fall in love with, and Timothy was the fantasy. Five years ago, when she became married, she neglected Timothy for some time until the couple started to have arguments. Once a pleasant fantasy, the demon twisted into a hateful being. The wife's relationship with her husband was damaging her internally, and as a result, both inward and outward aspects of her suffered. Finally, Timothy remembered one night how there was chanting, light and pain. He remembered hearing her screaming. He remembered being ripped apart from her.

"They both have scars," Sandra finished.

"Hm," I looked back to the closet. Though I didn't see anything, I knew he was there. "What about the other demon?" I looked at Sandra.

"There's another demon?" She asked.

At this point, science had done all it could. Now I had to go with my instinct. "Let's sleep in here tonight," I told Sandra.

I went downstairs and turned on every light I could. I felt hostility and fear. The feeling of bandages wrapping around me almost made it hard to breathe. As long as I kept myself focused on my task, I thought, I would make it before anything happened. The entire time I was out of the empty room upstairs, I felt something behind me. I knew it was the bandaged figure. I grabbed an armful of blankets and pillows, then just as I turned, I heard something clatter in the living room. I hollered out in surprise and peeked over to see what it was. A stack of boxes fell over nearby the box of books I looked through before. I clenched my teeth, turned off the bedroom light and hurried to the lit room of safety. I could still feel bandages wrapping around me. 'It's all in my head,' I assured myself. That's all demons were, powerful manifestations of the mind. If I just forgot about the bandaged creature, it couldn't do anything to me.

Another loud thud behind me had me cry out again. I turned off the light to the living room and ran upstairs, careful not to trip over the blankets. No wonder the couple felt uneasy. The claustrophobic, tense feeling I got the entire time I was in the house was borderline maddening.

Once I got into the empty room, I tossed the pillows and blankets on the floor and closed the door behind me.

"Daddy?" Sandra looked up at me.

"It's okay Sandra. We're okay in here," I turned my gaze

THE PAINTER AND OTHER STORIES

towards the closet. "I think."

I kept catching Sandra watching Timothy through the night. She was worried about him. I didn't have the heart to tell her that he would probably fade from existence by the time we were done. An exorcised demon, no matter how powerful, could stand to last for only so long after the ritual. It was painful to see a demon die that way, like watching an animal starve to death. Sandra could feel it, too.

The next morning, I took the liberty of cleaning part of the house. I left the basement alone, but the kitchen and living room were looking much better. "At least I feel less claustrophobic now," I muttered. Sandra spent most of the day in the room with Timothy, but I convinced her to help me with some of the living room. It took the entire day and there were still rooms that were horribly cluttered. The couple came home later that evening.

The husband, skeptical as ever, commented that at least I did some cleaning. I informed the wife what she needed to do. "First, you have to clean this house. Move furniture around, try new things. Fix the feng shui of the house."

"I've always been meaning to clean, but, between my husband's schedule and mine it's been difficult. Not to mention, we've both been feeling so drained being in this house."

"Well that's part of the problem. I didn't say it would be easy, but I got a couple rooms started for you and if you could afford me, you could always hire someone to clean it for you. Then you could start from scratch and then just keep at it."

"So that's it then? Clean the house?"

"Well, no," I admitted. "You've been having trouble with a demon in your past, haven't you? Something that was good at first, but started to get more self-destructive once you were married."

The wife looked taken aback. "I, well, admittedly I used to have a sort of problem similar to that but I've fixed that months ago."

"Whenever a person is stabbed or impaled," I replied. "Pulling out the object could cause more damage. You can't force something out without ending up with scars."

The wife put a hand to her heart. She looked down for a moment before straightening her posture. "So," The wife took a deep breath. "What do you think I should do?"

"I think you should talk to someone," I admitted. "Take therapy or confide in a group of close friends. Maybe try couple's therapy too."

"Are you insinuating something about my marriage," The wife warned.

I held out my hands, "All I know, ma'am, is that you have a damaged soul and a part of that soul is dying. It's too late for Timothy, he's been exorcised. But you don't have to live the rest of your life with that empty part of you. You still have the chance to heal, whatever it takes."

I saw the wife tense when I mentioned Timothy. She looked off to the side, her breathing got heavier.

"I don't recommend an exorcism as a solution for most cases. It's too abrupt and drastic a decision to not have consequences. Even so, if there's one done, make sure you bless the house afterwards. Otherwise, you end up with a job half done and other demons can come to try and get what they can from the aftermath."

"He's still around?"

"Not for long," I assured her. "But you have to talk about how you feel and try to work on healing internally. Otherwise, nothing will get fixed. Also, trust me with the cleaning. It'll make you feel better."

The wife looked skeptical, but she nodded. She must have thought that it was too bizarre for me to know about Timothy to not know what I was doing. I took my payment from her and said goodbye.

When I went upstairs to take my daughter, she was sitting in the closet, crying.

"Sandra?" I knelt beside her. "What's wrong?"

She couldn't answer me. I held out my arms and she hugged me. I picked her up to carry her to the car. I didn't see or feel anything in the room anymore. I glanced towards the closet again, but there was nothing there. I had hoped Timothy wouldn't disappear so soon.

"It's okay, Sandra. You did great. These things happen."

Sandra didn't feel like talking the rest of the night. She fell asleep in the car again on the drive to a hotel. I can't deny that I also feel bad about Timothy. Fear does horrible things sometimes. I didn't blame the wife to wish to be free from her personal demons.

I glanced over to my daughter. Her eyelids were puffy from

crying, her hair falling over her face. I smiled, thinking about how much I loved Sandra, but then the smile faded when I thought about what I must put her through taking her with me to work during her school holidays. I thought about how bad of a parent I must be. No matter what, I always seem to go back to these thoughts.

Sometimes, a personal demon can be pretty hard to bear.

THE HANGING MAN

My son Justin wasn't the type of child to have much of an imagination. When other children were busy playing house or pretending to have powers and imaginary friends, my son was throwing and catching his baseball around or playing tag and red rover. He wasn't very fascinated with cartoons or music. He liked watching baseball or cooking with me. He liked to spend time with people, but when it was time to go home, it was just me and my little guy. I always asked Justin about school, then I would listen to him talk while we cooked dinner together.

Justin was always a practical kid, never very imaginative. That's why I became alarmed when he said he saw a man hanging upside down at school one day. My heart froze. "Why was the man hanging upside down?"

Justin shrugged. "It was scary. I stayed away from him."

"Did you tell any of the teachers?"

"I did, but he was gone before I could show them."

"Was he," I started. I didn't want to scare Justin. "Awake when he was hanging upside down?"

"He looked at me, I think, and said 'hello,'" Justin replied. "Then I ran away."

"Let me know if you see him again, okay Justin? Stay away from him."

Justin agreed and we finished making dinner before sitting together to watch some baseball before bed.

The following day, Justin ran inside and threw his backpack on the ground.

"Justin, don't leave your backpack in the middle of the living room. How many times do I have to say that?"

"Mom, the guy was there again," Justin replied.

I forgot what he was talking about for a moment, but when my mind pulled me back to the man hanging upside down, I placed my hand on Justin's arms. "Did he try to do anything?"

"He was still floating upside down," Justin replied. "My friend Hank was there too but he said he didn't see him."

"Wait, Justin. Did you say he was floating?"

Justin looked up at me and nodded. "Yeah, he's all white, wears a baseball cap and just floats there upside down. He looked at me and said 'hello, Justin,' but when I pointed at him to Hank, he thought I was joking but he was really scary."

"Justin," I hesitated. "Do you think that maybe you could be imagining him?"

Justin shook his head. "Why would I make him up?"

"Well it's true that you never just make things up, but sweetie, a white floating man with a baseball cap is usually something that would be made-up." Justin looked hurt, as though he was about to cry. "Tell you what, I'll go to school with you tomorrow and you point him out to me. When do you usually see him?"

"At lunchtime," Justin admitted. "But mom, if you come to school the other kids might make fun of me."

"Well we might have to make that sacrifice Justin, if there's potentially a man lurking at your school that knows your name. Would you rather be embarrassed or be kidnapped?"

After a long pause, Justin answered, "I'll have to think about it."

The following day, I took some time off work to see my son during lunch. He played during the whole recess period, and when it was time for him to go inside, he said, "The man never showed up." Justin pointed to the outside bleacher seats for students that want to eat outside. "He's usually over there."

"Go on to class," I told him. "I'll go speak with the principal."

"But he's really there, mom!" Justin cried. "You don't believe me?"

The fear on my child's face made me upset and angry. To think that something was threatening my son had me mortified and furious. "Of course, I believe you, Justin. Don't worry, we'll figure this out. Just go to class, I'll take care of it."

I stormed to the principal's office and opened the door without hesitation. "My son is complaining that there's a strange man during recess that calls out to him."

"Well hello miss McMullen, nice to see you too. I'm sorry, what's this about a man?" The principal placed her hands onto her desk, papers beneath them. She smiled towards me.

"Why has nothing been done about the man harassing my child?" I demanded. The principal seemed confused.

"We have staff out in the playground every recess. I haven't been told about any man," The principal straightened in her seat.

"What does he look like? Where was he?"

The principal gestured me to a seat, and though I walked over to the chair I couldn't convince myself to do more than lean against it. "I haven't seen him myself, but Justin says that he wears a baseball cap, and he hangs by his ankles near the outside bleacher seats. He knows my son's name."

"Hanging by his ankles?" The principal looked skeptical. "Do you think maybe Justin might be imagining him?"

"My son never imagines anything," I informed her. "He's never played pretend or lied about something this serious in his entire life."

"Miss McMullen," The principal shifted in her seat. "I don't mean to pry... Whenever you come visit me, you're always alone. Where is Justin's father?"

I felt a surge of anxiety run up my spine. After a moment, I noticed that I had stopped breathing, so I let it out with a steady sigh. "He hasn't been a part of Justin's life in years, but I don't see how that can be involved with this situation."

"Well, it isn't uncommon for boys Justin's age to develop certain scenarios when they feel as though they have suffered some sort of loss. It isn't abnormal for a boy like Justin, who has unfortunately had no relationship with his father, to make up a sort of delusion of a person paying attention to him whenever he feels lonely. Of course, a report of strangers in this school is nothing to take lightly. I'll ask the other students if they've seen this man, but I also suggest, for Justin's sake, that he take a few courses of counseling."

"My child doesn't need counseling," I assured her.

"That might be true," The principal countered. "Still, isn't it worth it to see if Justin may need to talk to someone? It may help him if it turns out he needs it."

"If there's anything he needs to talk about, he can talk to me," I replied. After a few seconds of silence, I added, "But I'll think about it." I didn't want to be reminded of Justin's father. I didn't want to think about him ever again. However, the principal seemed concerned and I knew there was counseling offered to students for free. There really wasn't anything to lose. "You'll still investigate regardless though, right?"

"Of course," the principal assured me. "We want the children to be safe at school, if there's someone lurking around, I want to know about it."

I went home and prepared some lunch. I tried to get my mind off of everything, but there was something nagging at the back of my head. Justin always looked so afraid when I mentioned he may be imagining it. To be honest, I was also a little scared. Justin wouldn't remember, I thought, but his father had some very serious problems with hallucinations. I worried that my son may be showing signs of the same thing. I thought of the fighting and shouting and how Justin's father would always swear that there were terrifying creatures everywhere. The thought chilled me. It might sound as though I'm a terrible mother, but I almost hoped that the man with the baseball cap was a real person. At least then, the man could be arrested and my boy would be safe.

Once Justin came home, he hurried upstairs to his bedroom. I was contemplating on how to speak with him about the counseling when I heard him cry out and run downstairs. "He's in my room!"

Without any second thought, I rushed upstairs. I ran past him and rushed the room in question, but I didn't see anyone there.

I checked behind the door, the closet, and under the bed. I looked inside Justin's toy box. I looked outside. I went to every room on the second floor, and every place I could think of. There was no sound of footsteps, there were no open paths or windows, there wasn't even a bark from our lazy bloodhound Browley who slept on the living room couch. No matter where I searched there was no sign of a man anywhere in the house. I met Justin back in his room.

Justin gripped my shirt. I looked down to him, he kept his eyes near his closet, which I already checked. It unnerved me to see my son so upset, but I imagined this would be the best time to tell him. "Justin," I knelt beside him. "The principal and I have been talking, and we think that maybe, until we can find out about this hanging man, that you should talk with the school counselor once a week."

"Mom, I'm not crazy! I saw him, he was really there!"

"I know that, Justin. But just for a little bit, just to make me feel better, why don't we go tomorrow to set up an appointment-," Justin took a few steps back from me.

"I thought that out of everyone, you would believe me."

I felt a stab of pain in my chest. "The principal promised she would ask the other students if they have seen anyone."

"They'll just lie, everyone at the school hates me," Justin

muttered. "You think I'm crazy just like dad."

I felt a rise in my chest and my hands balled into fists. I was concerned and angry, it built up in me. "Don't talk to me like that young man, I am your mother. You are going to see the counselor and you are going to talk to them, is that clear?"

Justin turned away and slammed the door to his room. "Just for that, you're grounded for the rest of the night! No video games, it's homework, dinner and right to bed with you!"

I heard him yell something, but I didn't hear what he said. I went downstairs to cook and to turn off the internet of the house so he couldn't sneak online. The hour of cooking helped me calm down, but I still couldn't bring myself to talk to him about the hanging man. Why did he bring up his father all of a sudden?

Justin wouldn't speak to me during dinner. I didn't force him. I figured that he needed some time to think. The next day, we met the school counselor who tried to assure me that everything was going to be fine, but Justin had been quiet all morning. I left, hoping to get on with my chores without thinking about it. Tomorrow was the weekend. I thought about taking Justin somewhere fun to calm him down. I wondered if there were any baseball games being played nearby. The season was almost over so it would be a treat to watch a game together.

I got a phone call at work. I excused myself for a minute and went somewhere quiet to answer. It was the school's number and my heart froze.

"Miss McMullen," The principal inquired. "Are you busy?"

"No, not at all," I lied. "What's going on?"

"Well, we've spoken to the other students about the man Justin has been seeing, but no student can recall any strange man hanging by his ankles. My assistant went the extra mile to look through the footage caught by the security camera and… Well, I can show you if you'd like. It shows Justin shouting towards the bleachers, but there's no one there. The bleachers are completely barren."

"So you're positive that it's all my son's imagination," I asked. I was partly relieved, but also nervous.

"It does seem that way. The counselor wants to have a word with you at your earliest convenience."

I took a moment to think. The weekend was tomorrow, but could I take off from work again at such short notice?

It took me a moment to decide. "I'll be there in about an hour."

Usually I get off work just as Justin is getting out of school, so I'm home by the time he gets home. But if I'm going to be talking to the counselor, I'd rather it be while Justin is in class. I promised to work extra hours on Sunday to make up for what I've lost and hurried to the elementary school.

The counselor was a thin, balding man with an inviting smile. When I arrived, his smile seemed less genuine than usual. I didn't know if it was because of my anxiety or his. "Miss McMullen, as a counselor I cannot mention what was said between myself and your son," The counselor informed me. "But due to this alarming circumstance, I feel as though I must ask you a few questions."

I was hesitant, but I nodded.

"What can you tell me about Justin's father?" He began.

I bowed my head. I anticipated the question, but I was afraid of it all the same. I had rehearsed how I would reply while I was in the car, but my emotions made it hard for me to recall what I planned to say.

"He was a boyfriend of mine. We weren't together long. He was mean, hateful, abusive... Last I heard, he was being treated in a sanitarium."

"What for?"

My eyes met the counselor's. "He would have hallucinations. Sometimes they were so bad, he would come after me. He wouldn't see me... But Justin has never even been the sort of boy to imagine anything. He's very logical for a kid."

"Does Justin know anything about his father?"

"He was four years old when his father came to visit for the last time. He broke the restraining order to yell at me in front of my son about shadows with eyes and train whistles or whatever. I called the police and had him taken away, but Justin was really scared about it. He kept thinking his father would break into the house, I had to have him sleep in my room with me for nearly a month. It's the only time they ever met."

The counselor put a hand to his chin. "Have you two ever talked about it?"

"Of course not," I dismissed. "Why scare my son further? I told Justin to just forget about him. He was four years old, he probably doesn't even remember."

The counselor nodded. "Miss McMullen, I'm really sorry that you and your son had to go through such a difficult time. But I'm afraid visual hallucinations like Justin has could be hereditary. It's likely a symptom of a disorder."

"But why is he going through this now?" I demanded.

"No one knows, it could be something at school or a buildup of emotions over time, or the condition could just not have manifested until now. I suggest that he continues to see me, but perhaps if the hallucination doesn't resolve itself with therapy, we'll have to look at medicinal treatments. I could send a referral to your family doctor, but we'll see how therapy does first."

"Sir," I pleaded. "Is my son going to be okay?"

The counselor put a hand on my shoulder. He gave me another smile, but this time, it was genuine. "I chose this job because I wanted to help children. I will do everything that I can to make sure Justin is going to be okay." My shoulders relaxed, and I nodded my head.

I waited for Justin to get out of school and drove him home. He still didn't seem too keen on talking to me. "How was school?" I asked as we headed home.

"Fine," Was his reply.

"Did you learn anything new?" I asked.

Justin shrugged.

"Justin, you know you can talk to me about anything, right? Your mother has got your back. You'll talk to me if something's wrong, won't you?"

"Sure," He replied.

I didn't want to press him any further. I tried to change the subject. "So, I hear the Rangers are going against the Mocking Jays in a home game. It's their last game of the season. If you want, I can try to get us tickets for tomorrow."

That brightened him up immediately. "Really? We can go to an actual game?" He cried.

I laughed, "Absolutely! It's about time we root the Rangers in person against their rivals. Maybe we'll be some good luck for them."

Everything seemed to be back to normal. We did Justin's homework, had dinner, watched some television, then went to bed. I went on my laptop to order the tickets for tomorrow when I realized I still hadn't turned the internet back on. I got up and headed downstairs to the router when I heard Justin talking in his room as I passed.

"What do you want?" He whispered. "Well that's none of your business. Leave me alone or I'll tell my mom."

I swung open the door. Justin jumped and spun his head my way when before he was looking towards his closet. "Who are you talking to, sweetie?" I asked. Justin didn't say anything, but I walked over to look inside his closet. Nothing was there. I turned to see Justin was looking wide-eyed at me. I tried to offer him a smile. "We have to wake up early tomorrow. Try to get some sleep, okay?"

Justin nodded, first slowly, then stronger. "Okay mom."

His eyes darted left to the closet. I followed his line of sight. I turned back to him, then walked up and kissed his forehead. "I love you, sweetie."

"Love you too, mom," He replied. Justin laid back down and put the covers over himself. I left him in his room, closed the door and walked downstairs. On my way back upstairs, I heard him.

"Why are you hanging upside down?"

The next morning, I woke Justin up bright and early to take the drive to the game. "Go go Rangers Let's go," I chanted. It got him excited and he sprung out of bed to get dressed. We had to drive nearly two hours, but once we got there, we both felt a lot of energy. The game was fun, as expected. It was Justin's first time being there in person. I got us hot dogs and soda and we cheered until our throats were sore. The Mocking Jays won and Justin was upset, but I bought a baseball from the souvenir booth and we went down together to get it signed by his favorite players, who were more than happy to give signatures to their fans. Justin gushed at the Ranger's short stop, Jenny McMann. She was his favorite player. Harold Balter was the pitcher and he even gave Justin his baseball cap. "Keep cheering and keep dreaming," Harold told him. Justin was near tears he was so excited. We talked about it all the way home, and Justin never took the hat off the rest of the day.

I was satisfied to not hear any talking in Justin's room later that evening. He was so tired that he probably went straight to bed. I was close behind.

I was alone in the house. I was making lunch in the kitchen when I heard a familiar chuckle from behind me. My spine tensed and I didn't want to turn around. "William. How did you get out of the sanitarium?"

"Where's Justin?" He asked. I turned around.

"He's at school, and you're not going to see him again. He's afraid of you."

"What about you?" He asked. "Are you afraid of me?"

The figure before me was like a paper cutout, purely white and almost luminescent. His body faced me while his face was profile, his mouth wide, grinning so wide it could be to his ears. He hung by his ankles, or rather floated there. Nothing was suspending him. The outline was all I could see, the rest of him was whited out. There was a bill protruding from his forehead, as though he was wearing a baseball cap.

"I'm not afraid of you," My voice shook. "You're not real. This isn't real." I must be dreaming. That was it, I had to wake myself up.

"Falling," He said.

"What?"

"Falling. Falling. Falling," He repeated over and over. His sick, inhuman grin widening with every time he spoke. "Falling. Falling. Falling."

"Stop it!" I felt my chest rise. It was hard to breathe. It was getting harder to talk. "Just..." I ran. My body felt heavy, I kept trying. I couldn't go further than a crawl. I kept trying to crawl up to Justin's room. I tried to scream at myself, to tell myself to wake up. I kept hearing William's voice. "Falling. Falling. Falling."

The door to Justin's room was wide open. I gripped the doorframe and dragged myself to look inside just in time to watch my son standing on the window-frame of his room. I tried to scream at him, but only a whisper came out. I watched in horror as Justin's body tilted forward and plummeted down head first."

"AAAAAAAAAAH!" I felt myself falling until 'thud,' I hit the floor and I jolted awake. It was the dead of night, but I didn't care. I got up with shaky knees and rushed to Justin's room. When I swung the door open, Justin jumped out of bed.

"Mom?!" He cried. "What's wrong?'

It took me a couple seconds to calm my heart. Poor Justin looked mortified, seeing me stand there panting at his doorway. My screaming probably woke him. I swallowed. "Nothing, Justin. I'm sorry. I just had a nightmare."

Justin's shoulders relaxed, "I'm okay mom."

I sniffed and wiped the tears from my eyes. "Right. Yes, you are," I sighed. I walked over to him and hugged him tight. "I love you so much, Justin."

"Mom?" He fell silent for a couple seconds. "I love you too, mom."

I apologized for waking him up and then left him alone to go to sleep. I went downstairs to calm my shaking hands. I didn't like to stay in the kitchen at night, so I quickly grabbed a soda instead of bothering with a glass of water. I went to the living room and turned on some television. It took me an hour before I felt tired again. I had to go to work again in two hours, so I set my phone alarm and took a nap on the couch. Browley slept on my legs, giving me some comfort.

I had a babysitter come by every Sunday. It was a young high school kid that lived down the street. He knocked on the door ten minutes before I had to leave, and Browley barked to greet him. "Shhhh Browley," I scolded. I answered the door to let the babysitter in. "Good morning, Zach."

"Morning Lauren," He grinned. "Is Justin sleeping still?"

"Yes, he's still in his room," I replied.

"I bought a new video game, it's two-player and I think he'll like it," He showed me the cover. It looked like a battle warfare game. "Is this okay to play with him?"

"Mmh," I looked at the cover art. It seemed violent, but the rating wasn't too mature. Justin and Zach weren't violent kids, I trusted Zach's judgment, he'd been babysitting Justin for almost two years. "I suppose it's alright," It was reassuring to know Zach played with Justin while I was gone. At the very least, Justin wouldn't be left alone upstairs. I thought about the nightmare I had again.

"I'll see you around seven, I left twenty dollars on the counter for you to order dinner if you want and you can keep the change. Thanks for staying a little longer Zach."

Zach shrugged, "No worries, I like hanging out with Justin. Plus, I get some time to catch up on homework."

After a few hours at work, I forgot about the nightmare and managed to focus on what I had to do. Being an HR customer service representative for a large insurance company wasn't the most interesting job, but it paid well and I could stay in a cool building while it was nearly boiling outside. 'It shouldn't be this hot, it's supposed to be fall,' I sighed. Temperature was supposed to plummet next week.

Plummet.

I jumped when the phone rang. I nearly dropped it when I picked up the receiver. "Thank you for calling HR, this is Laura McMullen speaking."

I could hear Browley barking as I parked at our driveway. I felt so bad having Zach stay for twelve hours so I stopped by the bank to give him an extra ten bucks on top of the ten per hour I paid him. I walked in to see that Zach cleaned the living room and kitchen up a bit. There was pizza on the counter and Zach sat on the couch playing the game he brought over. "Zach, where's Justin?"

"Oh, he's," Zach looked upstairs. "He said he wasn't feeling well later this afternoon so I let him go upstairs to rest."

"Not feeling well?" I hurried upstairs to see if he was alright. I stopped in front of his door.

"Why shouldn't I open the window?"

I sprung open the door to see Justin in front of the window, wide open. My mind halted for a second. "Justin get away from the window!"

He was startled and confused, but he jumped back. "I needed some fresh air," He tried to explain.

I hurried over and closed the window. After a second of relief, I turned to see Zach at the doorway. I walked over and handed him his cash. "Here you go Zach. Thanks for staying an extra couple of hours. I put an extra ten in for you."

"Oh, thanks a lot," He replied. He took a glance over at Justin. "See you later bud," He waved and headed home.

I turned to Justin who seemed confused. I relaxed my shoulders. "Zach said you weren't feeling well."

Justin fidgeted, "Just a headache, and my stomach."

I felt his forehead. "You might be coming with a fever. I'll get the thermometer."

Justin had a small fever, so I decided to have him home from school Monday. Since Zach would be at school, I had to call a friend to see if she would watch him for the six hours I'd be at work. I gave him some medicine to help him sleep and went to bed.

"Falling. Falling. Falling."

My eyes were glued to the ceiling. Something woke me up, but I didn't know what. I heard something from the hallway, like something fell over. I sat up, grabbed the baseball bat in my room, and crept to Justin's room to make sure he was alright. Once I opened the door, I dropped my bat.

Justin stood on the windowsill, holding onto the frame. His head pointed down.

"Justin!" I screamed. I ran up to him as fast as I could.

"Huh?" He mumbled. He opened up his eyes and in his surprise he let go of the frame. He screamed and tried to turn to go inside or grab the window-frame again, but his body was tilting out the window.

I grabbed his arm tightly and pulled, wrapping my other arm around his waist. I pulled him towards me and held him close. We were both crying. "What were you doing?!" I demanded. "Trying to jump out the window, you could have died, Justin!"

"Ah-I don't know," He sniffed. "I was sleeping and then you screamed and I was at the window, I don't know mom, I was dreaming and…"

I held him tightly, my precious son. I didn't want to let him go. His body was so hot; his fever was probably worse. Was he sleep-walking? The large white moon shone a spotlight onto us from the open window. I took off his baseball cap to feel his forehead again. His cheeks were red and tear-stained.

"I'm crazy, aren't I mom? I'm crazy just like my dad."

"What?" I looked him in the eye. "Justin, you're not crazy."

"I am crazy," He insisted. "All the kids at school say I'm crazy and they're right, I'm gonna go to a crazy house like dad."

"Justin," I cooed. "They're not called crazy houses, and you're not going anywhere. How do the kids at school know about your dad, anyway?"

"Teresa at school says her dad works at a crazy house and she said he takes care of dad, and she said my dad is crazy and mean and she tells the other kids to stay away from me."

"How long has this been going on?"

Justin shrugged.

"Why didn't you tell me before that she was doing this?"

Justin shrugged again.

I took Justin downstairs and took out some cookies and milk. Browley barked at the living room window at some squirrels. "Browley," I scolded and gave him a treat to be quiet.

Justin sat at the table, his breath ragged. He dipped a cookie into his drink, sniffing and wiping his eyes with the palm of his other hand.

I sat across from him. "Justin," I said. "The thing about your father... He sees things that aren't there. But that doesn't make him crazy. He's just sick, and he's at the sanitarium to get help."

Justin took a bite of the cookie, and I continued, "Just because your father is sick, it doesn't mean you are too. And even if you were, if you just tell me, we can take care of it. With the bullying at school and with any hallucinations you have or anything else, you can always tell me."

"I didn't want to play pretend because I thought that if you thought I was seeing things then you would take me to the place dad went."

"Oh, Justin, sweetheart," I felt my heart break. Was I the reason he never played with the other kids? I felt like a horrible mother. "I would not let you be taken away from me like that, I promise. We could get you some therapy and try some medicine if we needed but I promise I would never send you away. No matter what you see or who you talk to, I will always be there for you. As long as you're safe and sound."

Justin sniffed and nodded, eating his cookies. I felt myself nearly ready to burst into tears seeing my poor boy so worried, above all, that I would just send him away. I swore I would do what I could to talk to the school about the bullying, and not only would I let the counselor be there for him to talk to, but I would be there too, whenever Justin needed me.

Browley started barking again.

"Quiet down, pup," I told him. Browley kept barking. I looked over to him. "Browley, I told you to s-."

I jumped out of my seat.

"What is it, mom?" Justin asked, looking out the window.

I kept looking at the window for a few more seconds before responding, "Nothing, Justin. Just thought I saw someone."

I didn't want to let him know that, just as I looked over, I saw a white blur with the silhouette of a man plummeting face first to the ground from the window. There was no thud, there was no evidence except Browley's barking which stopped the second I stood from my seat. It was the last time I saw the hanging man, and I hope it was the last time for Justin, as well.

THE PAINTER AND OTHER STORIES

RUSTY

When you wake up in the darkness and your body is still fast asleep, your eyes and ears will hallucinate what might be lurking around you. Many people can recall this happening once or twice, but few people experience this sensation regularly. In my case, however...

I have lived in haunted houses before. I am sure that most people hold disbelief in such things until they've experienced it themselves. I was never a stranger to the idea of waking nightmares, but I had never had them happen as common as when I lived on the house by the abandoned farm. The house had been refurbished. It experienced just a little bit of fire damage from the flames that obliterated the old farmland. It happened recently, so not only was there nothing growing around the property but the home I had rented was incredibly cheap. I have since moved out of that house.

Despite the dead land, a wild rooster crowed in the morning. I could hear the sweet, humming of the trains at night. Not many people bothered me, and that was just fine. I was never very social to begin with. The first week I moved in, the train whistle put me to sleep. The sound of the wheels rolling on the ground followed me to my dreams, but though I had expected to move on to a different scene there was just the train, and it was getting louder. It kept on hissing and chugging until the whistle became deafening. I opened my eyes.

The house was dead silent. I tried to calm my breathing, but I was confused. I never experienced something like that in my dreams before. I laid back down and tried to sleep.

Ever since that night, I would have frequent waking nightmares. Twice or maybe three times a week, I would wake up paralyzed, watching my door open, listening to people moving around in my house, witnessing small crawling shadows drag its way to my bed. One night, a haggard old woman laughed maniacally as she bobbled her head right next to mine. Her smile was permanent, with few teeth to present. Her white hair fell thinly over her wrinkled, decaying scalp. I tried to scream, but nothing came out. I had to watch. I had no other choice. Eventually, I would be able to whine or mumble or move, and instantly the images and sounds would cease to exist.

You would think that this sort of inconvenience would be enough to make someone move out. You would surmise that anyone with a dose of sanity would deem this situation too much to stand and find a new place to live. However, I didn't mind too much. I could live my life occasionally being woken up by the startling sight of a dark visitor. I conceded to live in this haunted house full of demons and the occasional sleepless night. The vision of Rusty, however, was what made me change my mind.

I woke up not to a sound or a vision, but due to the feeling of light pressure. I thought it could be a bug. I whimpered.

"Sssssshhhhhhh."

I struggled to open my eyes. I wished that I just went back to sleep. A pale face with two eyes, wide apart from each other and too small for the face it was attached to, stared at me. It was unblinking. It was only two eyes, nothing else. The neck was long and craned down at me from its massive, nude body beside me. I whined again, trying to scream.

"Sssssh it's okay," I heard it say. There was no mouth to move. It hunched over my head with its hand preoccupied with holding a needle. The tip of the needle was pressed against my temple. I felt my body tingle, I tried to scream, to get it to disappear, but it just stood there. I don't know if it was taking or applying something into my head, but its voice and presence, though unreal and alarming, kept me too calm to scream and too tired to thrash around.

This happened twice while I lived in that house. I can still feel the pressure against my temple. What did it want? I named him Rusty, perhaps as an attempt to name something terrifying to make it less scary. I have so many questions that I don't think I'll ever know the answer to. Why did I get so many night terrors in that house alone? Who was Rusty? What was he doing with the needle? Was all of this really in my head? I hope so. But I do know that, ever since moving out of that house, I never saw Rusty again.

THE DIMENSION TRAIN

In the dead of night when living man sleeps and the nocturnal creatures trail the blackness of their world and rustle the still leaves, the silence of the old cities and humble fields is pierced with the gentle hum of a train whistle. The mighty beast gasps its rhythmic breath as it pushes forward through the darkness. This train calls the passengers forward from abandoned and unfinished tracks, it finds someone with its haunting call and lures them in with the bright light of the car, warm and welcoming, an angler fish in the silent abyss.

The passenger wakes alone in the car, confused and afraid. "Where am I going," They often wonder. The conductor appears, his pale, blank face graced only with a gray smile. His appearance is otherworldly, contrast to his fashion of pinstripe suit, complete with fedora and cane.

He introduces himself as Jazzer, and there are two places to go. He points to the front of the train, and then to the back. "This train goes two ways. One is your destination, and the other is *not* your destination." His grin widens at his passenger's distress.

There are stories where an option is made and the passenger finds themselves in a completely different world. Other stories claim to have the passenger arrive home, but who is to say? For those said to stay in the cart, well... No one knows what comes of them.

From dimensions with small differences to vastly different existences, Jazzer takes his train, disguised as something average, notable only by its long, haunting cry and bright light. Some places see him often, others not at all. Some have stories of him to tell children at night, others may never hear of Jazzer or his train. But in every dimension, disappearances will happen. In every dimension, a being appears from the most barren of places hysterical and confused.

Late at night, the whistle blows. The train glistens like a chrome bullet, chanting its mantra as it continues from destination to destination. Where will you go?

THE UNLUCKIEST LUCK

Darla Penwell was a modest old woman. She stayed in the same small house for nearly thirty years. Before her husband passed away, they owned the house and the land around it, and she was too old and too sentimental to move away now. She would sometimes feel as though her husband was still with her. Her children and grandchildren visited often, and there were neighbors that would greet her, but she spent the better portion of her days crocheting and knitting or bending small strands of wire to design stunning jewelry. For most of it, she would sell it online with the help of her daughter Nora-Jean or use them as gifts for birthdays and holidays. There were very few pieces she would keep to herself, but when she did, she kept them in a large jewelry box her husband made for her before he passed.

She had a guest room fashioned with doilies and lace, but she hadn't had a guest spend the night in over ten years. She kept her scarves, sweaters and other projects in the room, waiting to be given or sold, made with love and care. Darla Penwell was excited for the holidays when the family would come for a meal and they can catch up on what is going on with everyone's busy lives. She would laugh and cook more food than anyone could finish and give the family her creations which she made with them in mind.

In the dark nights, Darla would have to admit that she missed her husband. He died of black-lung working in the mines, supporting his family and working long hours for little pay. Darla didn't miss her work in the fields and was thankful of her husband's luck which got them the land where they built their house.

In her eighties, Darla Penwell was faced with her economy's rapid decline. Her medicine became more expensive, as did food and insurance. Her unemployment and her small revenue from her hobbies became no longer enough, and one night she sat in the dim light of her kitchen table, going through her papers and realizing that she may have no other choice but to sell the house.

Down the hallway, she thought she saw something move. She looked up to what she thought looked like burlap, fashioned to look like a man wrapped inside. Darla gasped, but it slowly faded from sight as her eyes adjusted. She took off her glasses and cleaned them off. "Lord I am too old to be up this late at night," She muttered. Darla stood from her table and shuffled down the hallway to bed.

She had a hard time sleeping. She kept thinking that there was someone watching her. She tried to convince herself that it was her husband checking up on her. Something about this feeling was different. She remembered how her husband used to always say, "I've got an angel of luck lookin' after me, 's why everything always works out. I always feel their presence when somethin' goes right." Could this be the angel of luck, maybe?

"Angel, if you're listenin'," she whispered. "Please help me keep this house. It's all I got left of Eunice in this whole wide world."

The next morning, Darla woke up to the phone ringing. It was an alien sound to her, since she hardly ever got phone calls. She reached for the cord phone on her nightstand. Her daughter responded.

"Momma, did you look at your store, yet?"

"Honey, I haven't even woken up yet," Darla replied.

"Sorry to wake you, but you should look at your store website right now. Everything you had up there just sold out!"

Darla was still rubbing the sleep out of her eyes. "Alright, just let me wake up and I'll have a look." As she was about to tell her daughter that she'll call her back, Darla caught something again in the hallway. Once she turned her head, it was gone. "Nora-Jean, I'll call you back honey. I love you too," Darla hung up the phone and shuffled on her slippers to get her medication. Once she had brewed some coffee and made breakfast, she sat at the desk where Nora-Jean set up her computer.

Once she got to the website where her store was found, she was surprised to see every item say 'Sold Out' across the photo. She looked into her bank account and realized that, due to this huge boost of sales, she had enough money to last her for a few months at least. She put a hand to her chest. "My prayer was answered," She realized.

Darla had Nora-Jean come by to help her ship everything, and she spent the rest of the day celebrating with Nora-Jean and her family. Darla was glad to see her grand kids and son-in-law after so long. They went out to eat somewhere nice, which was something Darla hadn't done since a few years before. As they enjoyed each other's company, Darla decided to put the store on hold for a few months while she made more things to sell. She wasn't counting on another burst of sales like that, but she also felt silly having only one item in the store while it took days to make more.

The next day, she took a couple hours with some tan yarn and a small metal chain to knit the man-shaped figure she'd seen in the hallway. Darla had no fear of the being. She was aware that angels often looked terrifying in stories. If this truly was the angel she saw, then she wanted to have something to show she appreciated his luck. Moments after she finished, there was a phone call.

"Is this Darla Penwell?" A male voice she didn't recognize inquired.

"Yes, speaking. May I ask who is calling?"

"Mrs. Penwell, my name is Roger Dhoffer. I'm calling on behalf of the company I work for called 'Handmade's.' I wanted to speak to you about the things you've been selling on your personal store. Do you make all of these things?"

"Yes sir," Darla admitted. "But why would a company wanna speak to me?"

"To be honest, miss Penwell, we stumbled upon your small store and we wanted to have you make some products for our company. 'Handmade's' prides itself in offering talented people such as yourself a partnership. We would like to use your designs, specifically your jewelry, for our product. You'll be given royalties, of course. Could we perhaps meet you to talk about the specifics?"

"You wanna pay me for my designs?" Darla felt so overwhelmed, she didn't know what to say. "Well I don't know, never had nothin' like this happen to me before."

"I happen to live nearby," Mr. Dhoffer explained. "If you'd like, we can talk more in person so it isn't so overwhelming. Is your address on your website correct? I can visit you tomorrow."

Darla was always very fond of company. "Well, alright, if that is no trouble for you."

Darla called Nora-Jean immediately after getting off the phone with Mr. Dhoffer. Darla asked Nora-Jean if she would be willing to come by tomorrow when the businessman arrived. Nora-Jean hastily agreed. Once Darla had finished speaking with her daughter, she noticed she still had the little burlap figure in her hand.

Her daughter got there first. The two of them wondered what was going to happen to Darla's little knick-knacks. Nora-Jean knew her mother was in financial trouble, so she hoped this would lead to something worthwhile. Darla kept the little burlap angel keychain with her. Her daughter saw it, but didn't say anything. Nora-Jean knew her mother felt some significance to it if she went as far as to make it out of her precious yarn.

A man knocked on the door with a navy suit and a winning smile. He greeted the two women and Darla offered him to have a seat. "Thank you," He said. "I'm very excited to speak with the two of you, management is in awe with the detail you put in your jewelry, and how it's all handmade."

"What are you wanting to do with my momma's jewelry, sir?" Nora-Jean asked.

"Well, all the details are written down on this contract," Mr. Dhoffer admitted. "But of course, I'll explain anything that's difficult to read. Generally, 'Handmade's' would like to hire your mother to make more designs for them to duplicate and mass-produce for the public. For every item that's sold, Darla will get paid for it."

"How much?" Nora-Jean questioned.

"The item will be priced based on its cost to make and ship and advertise, plus a portion for us to profit and pay our employees, and then a portion given to you. Usually the way the profit for the item goes, 80 percent of the profit goes to the company and 20 percent will go to you."

"Nu-uh," Nora-Jean wagged her finger. "My momma gets at least 50 percent of the profit if she's gonna be working during her retirement to give you more things to sell."

"The profit is a little harder to split than that, I'm afraid. As much as I would love to do that, I would have to clear it with my superiors first. May I suggest a compromise, down the middle of the offers, of 35 percent?"

Darla reached into her purse and rubbed her thumb against the angel trinket.

Mr. Dhoffer's phone rang. "Excuse me," He apologized before answering the phone. "Yes ma'am. Actually, as luck would have it I'm here now. She seems interested, but inquiring about a 50 percent profit?" There were a couple moments of silence.

"Well, that seems fair. Let me fix that on the contract," Mr. Dhoffer took a pen and crossed out a few things and wrote some new numbers before saying farewell and hanging up the phone. Mr. Dhoffer was a good man who met a compromise with Nora-Jean and Darla in every part of the contract. As Darla signed, he caught a glimpse of the keychain. "Whoah," he exclaimed. "Is that creepy little guy something you made?"

"Why, yes," Darla admitted. "He's my little angel of luck."

Mr. Dhoffer chuckled, "If I met an angel that looked like that, I'd probably tell it to go away."

There was a small air of tension in the room, but none of the three that were present could tell where it came from. Nora-Jean took the earliest opportunity to change the subject. "Will you be wanting to stay for lunch, Mr. Dhoffer?"

"That's kind of you," He replied. "But I have some work to do still and I can't be enjoying such hospitality while on the clock." Mr. Dhoffer left the house. Nora-Jean and Darla looked at each other, both nervous and excited to see what this new contract will bring to Darla's life.

Days passed, and Darla had been working on more jewelry when she got a phone call. It was a different man who said he worked for 'Handmade's,' and he was wondering when to expect the first couple designs for next month. "I'll have them done in a couple days," She replied. "Is Mr. Dhoffer off today?"

"Mr. Dhoffer?" The man on the other line sounded hesitant. "Mr. Dhoffer, well, actually he's currently in the hospital."

"Oh no, what for?" Darla gasped.

"Just yesterday, after we finished what we needed for your paperwork, he went to his car to find his car wouldn't start. As he was walking around to see who could jump start his car, he got caught in a mugging. They hurt him pretty badly."

"Oh no, the poor boy," Darla lamented.

"Yeah, if his car's battery didn't drain out of juice, he wouldn't have been near that area to begin with. It was a lot of rotten luck."

Darla took the time to have Nora-Jean drive her to the hospital so they could give Mr. Dhoffer some flowers. His fiancé was with him when they got there, and she thanked them for their kindness. Darla kept the burlap man keychain in her purse.

Under the contract, Darla had to make four different types of jewelry a month. At home, she would work as much as she could to twist the wires and cover the gems. One afternoon before the end of the first month, one of Darla's neighbors came by for a visit.

"I heard that you had a deal with 'Handmade's,'" Wendy said as she sipped her tea.

"Yes, well, nothing has come of it so far, but we will see by the start of next month. Mr. Dhoffer was the gentleman that called to me. The poor thing, I hope he gets better soon. I believe he's able to go home next week."

"It's scary what happened to him, I remember Nora-Jean telling me about it. Do you suppose you'll still be making gifts for everyone? I don't mean to overwhelm you, but we all really love your presents every year. They're always so thoughtful and sincere."

"Oh, I'll certainly still be making presents, Wendy. Though they may be more of my knitting and crocheting than the wiring work jewelry."

"Have you made any new things with your knitting recently?" Wendy asked.

"Not for a while," Darla admitted. "The last thing I've made was a small trinket of my little angel of luck."

"Oh?" Wendy inquired. "May I see it?"

Darla took the little burlap man out of her purse. Wendy's face fell slightly. "Well, he's certainly not the cutest of angels, is he?"

"Most angels aren't," Darla reminded her. "Besides, he reminds me a little bit of Eunice."

Wendy's nose scrunched up. "That thing? Darla, why would it remind you of Eunice? That thing's positively frightening."

"I don't find it frightenin'," Darla admitted. "In fact, I think it's kinda cute. Like one of those creatures the kids are collectin' these days on the computer."

"Well Darla, if you like it so much. Though I still think you shouldn't show it off to many people. Other people might think you're losing your mind."

"I might be," Darla admitted. "But even if I was, what's the harm in keepin' this little angel?"

"I still think you should get rid of it," Wendy admitted. "It's just creepy."

"I can't."

The words surprised even Darla as she spoke them. It was so abrupt, and she hadn't even thought to say it. It came out desperate too, she thought. Her voice had cracked. Darla cleared her throat and tried again. "I can't just get rid of it, Wendy. It's been such a good little luck charm."

"It looks more like a demon than an angel," Wendy insisted.

"Well if you read the descriptions of the angels Wendy, you'll find yourself wonderin' 'What's the difference?'"

Wendy went home after they spent the afternoon together. Darla was glad she had company. It was so long ago since her last visit with her neighbors. Darla spent the rest of her day cleaning the house before going to bed for a long, restful sleep. She dreamed about Eunice. Her heart ached to see him again. He acted just like normal in the dream, working hard and playing with young Nora-Jean and spending his evenings with her in the comfort of the home they built together. They sat by the fire, though Darla began to wonder about the strange blue glow mixed with the red. After a moment, the fire was screaming.

Darla woke up in the early morning to the sound of sirens. There was a soft glow outside and she could smell smoke. Darla sprung out of bed as fast as she could. She was relieved for a moment to see that the fire department was going further down the road and that nothing on her property was on fire, but her chest leaped when she investigated to see Wendy's house in flames.

There was nothing an old lady like her could do, but she threw on some slippers and warmer clothes to at least make sure that Wendy was okay. She wasn't permitted anywhere near the house and was urged to go back inside. "But Wendy. Sir, please just let me know if everyone's okay."

He didn't say anything to her then, so Darla was left wondering the entire morning. She waited for the fire department and the ambulance to leave before she was able to go out to the crowd still waiting by. Wendy's two sons and her husband were getting ready to leave. Darla hurried towards them, and the husband waited for her to arrive.

"What happened? Is Wendy okay?"

The husband was hesitant. "We don't know. Wendy's in the hospital now, we're going to see her and make sure everything's taken care of."

Darla called Nora-Jean to pick her up and take her to the hospital again. Nora-Jean was devastated to hear that Wendy was in a fire. She called off work for the day for a family emergency and hurried to pick up her mother. They arrived at the hospital moments after Wendy was taken out of intensive care and placed into a room. Wendy's husband and two boys had been crying.

Nora-Jean laid down the flowers and sat with Wendy's family. Darla went through her purse for tissues and her hand brushed against the burlap figure.

Wendy didn't wake up in the time they were there. She was stable, so Darla and Nora-Jean promised to come visit again soon. The fire started in the master bedroom. Wendy slept beside the alarm clock which it was suspected the plug sparked and ignited the carpet. Wendy would need skin graphs and a respirator. Her lungs were damaged from the smoke.

Once Darla was home alone, she took a long look at the keychain. The little figure had no eyes, but she felt as though it was watching her. For the first time, she started to wonder. "First, Mr. Dhoffer. Then Wendy. Oh, Eunice, was this really your angel? Or have I stumbled into something sinister?"

The next day, she received her first paycheck from 'Handmade's.' She clutched her chest and nearly fainted. She called Nora-Jean who cried out in surprise. The first month made her over a thousand dollars. After the bills were paid, her first act was to give a few hundred to Wendy's husband to help pay for the house and Wendy's hospital visit.

There wasn't a day after that in which the angel wasn't on Darla's mind. She didn't want to think that there was any correlation, but she couldn't stop thinking about it. "Angel," She muttered to the little doll. "You didn't have anything to do with Wendy's house catching fire, did you? It ain't possible, is it?" Darla set the little thing down. "I hope not. You've been my little good luck charm. Are you even the same angel that Eunice used to boast about?" Darla looked behind her. She felt her heart race. The thought crossed her mind, 'If I tried to get rid of this angel, would the same thing happen to me?'

Late that night, Darla had a dream. She found herself surrounded by human-sized versions of the doll she made. She watched as Mr. Dhoffer became consumed by one, and Wendy was consumed by the other. Once they were wrapped into the yarn doll, their bodies kept floating and the doll turned from harmless yarn to full-grown figures, their large tongue-like tendrils hanging out from their diaphragm. Darla tried to run. She tried to scream. She turned to see her daughter, blank-eyed, being consumed by another yarn-made doll.

Darla shot up in bed, panting. It was dark and she couldn't

stand it. She turned on every light in her house. Whatever this apparent creature of luck was, she wasn't going to have it harm her daughter.

Nora-Jean came by to have lunch. Darla had the haunting angel in her fist. "Nora-Jean," Darla began. "You know the little doll I've been taking with me everywhere?"

Nora-Jean looked up from her food. "Yes, though I didn't want to bring it up. You said it was your angel of luck?"

"Well, it is lucky for me. But do you remember when Mr. Dhoffer talked bad about it? Days later, he went to the hospital. I hadn't told you, but before the fire Wendy and her family had, Wendy had come to have a visit, and she said some of the same things Mr. Dhoffer said. I think, Nora-Jean, that the doll might have some sort of curse."

"Momma," Nora-Jean laughed. "You made that little thing yourself. It's nothing but a little knitted keychain."

"But Mr. Dhoffer and Wendy. That can't be coincidence."

"Momma," Nora-Jean sighed. "If that creepy little thing does anything, it just makes people uncomfortable."

"Ssssh, Nora-Jean please don't say anything bad about the angel. I'm afraid you'll get hurt."

Nora-Jean put a hand on her mother's hand. "Momma, don't worry. If you wanna keep it, then keep it. But this little thing ain't going to be anything more than a silly little trinket."

Darla felt a chill up her spine. "Nora-Jean, I'm warning you. Please don't say anything negative to the angel."

"Momma, trust me, it's fine. There is no such thing as a vengeful angel of luck. It's just a thing you thought up one night when you were missing daddy, nothing more."

Darla was speechless. She was certain that the little angel was angry. "Nora-Jean," Darla cried. "What have you done?"

Darla was terrified that Nora-Jean was going to be hurt unexpectedly. Later that night, she held the little burlap man to her chest. Tearfully, beggingly, she said, "Please. Please don't hurt my daughter. I'll do anything you want just please don't hurt Nora-Jean."

Darla prayed all night long, the burlap doll clutched to her chest, until she fell asleep. The next morning, she didn't wake up. Even as 'Handmade's' called her, and even as Nora-Jean tried to call, there was no answer. Nora-Jean rushed to her mother's house to see she had passed away. Nora-Jean fell beside her mother's bed, sobbing and begging for her to wake up.

Darla Penwell was buried in a graveyard nearby. The house went to Nora-Jean who decided to keep it in the family. As they were going through Darla's old stuff, Nora-Jean stopped. "Huh."

"What is it," Her husband asked.

"Nothing much, it's only that," She sighed. "I haven't seen the little luck angel of hers since the last day I saw her." It's been months now since the funeral. Darla wondered what might have happened.

Nora-Jean caught a glimpse of someone in the reflection of a window behind her. She focused on it for a second before gasping and turning over. She could have sworn there was some beige-covered person behind her. Maybe she was just stricken with grief. She dismissed it as such and continued emptying the house.

GENEROUS OR PROSPEROUS

A man hangs by his ankles, smiling. It's unclear why he is smiling or who the smile is for. It's unclear why he is hanging by his ankles. The man named Hiroshi hangs there, grin swirled as whipped cream and outline bright as fresh paper. He hangs there, smiling, speaking to young children desperate enough to listen.

Hiroshi, meaning generous. Someone who gives abundantly, a man that offers solace to those in need. Hiroshi, meaning prosperous. Someone who is given an abundance, who lavishes in the consequences that life has given them. The story is that Hiroshi is a being that a child sees before the child falls to their death. Hiroshi, the omen. Attempting to call upon the parents, or anyone who will listen, for help. Hiroshi, the curse, luring the children to their eventual demise in order to gain what he does from the child's soul. It is unknown which path is true, or if they may both be true.

I wish I had listened to my little brother. I wish I had known before what was at stake. When Aidan told me that he saw a ghostly figure of a hanging man, I thought he was trying to scare me. He always had a habit of trying to scare me for no reason. One night, he just shouted on about how nobody ever listened to him. I thought he was being dramatic. I didn't think many people listened to me either, but I never whined about it. Aidan started spending less time bothering me and more time in his room, which I didn't complain about. I could get a lot more homework done when he was busy doing something else. Besides, if there was something really wrong, he'd tell our parents, I thought.

Aidan came into my room. He told me that only Hiroshi will ever know how he felt. I didn't know this friend of his, but then he told me again that it was the ghost that spoke to him. I had a thought that maybe my brother was going crazy. I told him that if he wanted to talk to someone so bad, he should talk to our parents. Really, I couldn't understand what his problem was.

I woke up that night to a scream outside my window. It took me a moment to gather that there was something wrong, but once I did, I hurried to my window to see what I could make out in the night. I saw my mother crying, looking at something closer to the house. Dad ran back inside to grab his phone. It looked like I could get a better view from it at Aidan's window, so I hurried over to see what mom was crying about.

I got into Aidan's room and thought, for a second, that I saw something fade away near Aidan's window. I hesitated, but walked closer. Aidan wasn't in his bed, and the window was wide open. I felt my heart throw itself against my chest. I noticed I was holding my breath, but my stomach was too upset to let it out. There, laying sprawled below, was my brother. I cried out before my father came from behind me and took me in his arms. I can't remember everything that happened, but I remember shaking and crying while clinging to my dad's arm.

There is not a day that passes that I don't think of things I could have done differently. I was so caught up in my own life that I never took my brother seriously. Whatever this vision that Aidan called Hiroshi was, I can never decide if it was a warning or a death sentence. There was one night where I saw the creature vividly. He smiled at me. His image morphed into that of my brother, falling head first onto the pavement below. The image haunts me. I wish things had turned out differently, but I suppose the warning signs were there, and I have no one to blame but myself.

GHOST IN THE ROAD

Sometimes I would go for a drink at the bar before driving my motorcycle home. I didn't drink much, just a couple of beers. If I was ever too drunk, I called a cab or had someone drive me home. One night, I just finished hanging out at the bar when I heard my friend Jerry say, "Hey Tamara, you good to drive home? Something's come up and I have to go now."

I wasn't ready to go yet, so I told him to go ahead and I would drive my motorcycle home, which meant that I had to start drinking soda and water. By the time my last game of pool was done, it was nearly 3 in the morning. I may have been a little buzzed, but I was more tired than anything. I hoped that I wasn't going to fall asleep on the road.

I took the back roads slowly. I didn't want to pass out on the highway so I tried driving through the less busy streets. It wasn't long before another motorcycle came up from behind me. They were coming up pretty fast, so I pulled to the left of the road to let them pass. They slowed down when I did. I motioned with my arm for them to just pass me, but they just kept behind me, lights blaring. I blinked to try and see the road better, but the motorcyclist kept tailing me. "What is his deal," I mumbled. I tried to check my mirror and see the face of the guy, but all I could make out was a black full-face helmet. At this late at night, I thought he was an idiot for wearing a helmet that would dim the lights, but it would explain why he'd have his brights on without knowing. I blinked my lights on and off to tell him.

He sped past me then, and I tried to focus ahead on the road in case he was some jerk trying to make me mad. He pulled in front of me, and I faltered for a second. My lights caught the glare of the glass on the rider's helmet. He was looking at me, I could tell from his helmet, but his head was twisted at 180 degrees. I cried out and stopped my motorcycle, and he sped off into the night.

I welcomed the silence. I heard nothing but my breathing and the rustling of small creatures in the woods beside me. Until a few seconds later, I heard a motor coming from behind me. I looked back, and to my terror, it was the same bike, the same helmet, the same rider. I watched as he sped past me, his head twisting as he overtook me to stare while he sped off. Then he came up from behind me again, the same rider. His head twisted and kept me in its sights, twisting to a sickeningly impossible angle.

I revved up my engine as quickly as I could. I had to drive out of there! I took a turn, but he took the same turn. His head twisted to watch me as he came by. I went down a narrow path, but he was still able to make it by me, still staring. I tried to ride faster so he couldn't pass me, but no matter how fast I went, he would still pass me. "Stop it!" I shouted at him. He kept coming from behind me.

I went into the highway, shaking and wide awake. I tried to keep a level head but I kept looking back in fear that he would come up from behind me. I was thankful that I lived close to the exit. Every time I heard an engine behind me or saw headlights, I panicked and kept my eyes forward. Every time, it was a car. I was hyper-focused on getting home, driving as straight as I could. I kept driving and thinking that he would show up until I got home. Maybe I lost him, I thought. Near my exit, the streets were dead, there wasn't a sound. I felt uneasy that there were no other drivers, but it made me relax that I was the only headlights on the road for a moment. I breathed a sigh of relief.

I pulled in towards the last street home when I heard the engine behind me again. I screamed and pulled into my driveway as fast as I could. I looked behind me to see the driver looking my way as he drove past but thankfully there were too many bushes to see if his head twisted to watch me still. I ran inside and locked all the doors and windows. I stood beside my front door with a crowbar in hand, waiting for the sound of his engine, but everything was silent. It was so calm, like how late nights should be. I barely slept that night. I kept waiting to see or hear the motorcycle which never came back. Part of me thinks it may have been the alcohol, but it would be impossible to have a hallucination that strong, right? That was the last night I ever drove home after drinking, and I never saw the motorcyclist after that.

MRS. RICKSON

Her husband was a marvelous painter. Mrs. Rickson was proud of how passionate he was for his work and for her. Ever since they were married, he painted beautiful portraits that everyone in town wanted to have. His pieces were always very vibrant and detailed. There was warmth and love in his pieces. Mrs. Rickson could feel his presence in each work. 'They are his children,' she would recall. It was what he would call them. For Mr. Rickson, all that mattered were his paintings and his wife.

Even before they were married, they were the only two things he cared for. However, his paintings weren't always as cheerful and full of love. Although he has had paintings that were gentle and sweet before, there were few of them. He was consumed with dark figures in his mind. Mrs. Rickson was frightened of her husband's old work, despite how she loved his passion for all of it. Their house was filled with works of knights and fairy-tale creatures and beautiful scenes with animals or lovely people doing everyday tasks. The dark paintings were left in the basement, which Mrs. Rickson never visited. She did not like to leave her room at night. She could hear scratching and creaking just outside, and their bedroom was the only place where she felt safe. She would feel the most peace in their bed beneath her favorite creation, 'Fairest Lady Tempera.' Her husband always told her that the scratching and creaking was only the house settling, but he could sense her apprehension.

"I promise, my love," Van Rickson assured. "You are safe in this house. The creature can't get you here."

The creature was a horrible monstrosity that murdered Mrs. Rickson's father. It had fur dark as oil and teeth and claws sharp as razors. It horrified Mrs. Rickson and haunted her dreams, but she felt safe with her husband who managed to fight it away from her and her brother years ago. She was always reassured by 'Fairest Lady Tempera' hanging at the headboard of the master bedroom that Van Rickson created to show his love for her. The painter's wife was in the image of an angel, sitting on a white wooden bench with her disheveled husband resting his head on her lap. They rested there under the tree on a hill where the two would often visit for picnics. She felt most fond of this piece. It had more than just his love, but specifically his love for her.

56

There were some nights where even the vision of the painting couldn't cast out the memory of the monster that murdered her father. "I am haunted by the creature, Van," She admitted to him one night. "What if it tries to come after you?"

"There hasn't been a sighting of it in years. It may have moved on since then. Besides, you will always be protected when you are with me."

Before they were married, Mrs. Rickson used to enjoy parties and gatherings with the townspeople. Now that she was with her husband and enjoyed his company more than anything else, Mrs. Rickson spent much of her time reading in the living room as her husband painted. She loved stories of every type, and she would share the stories with her husband when she thought he would enjoy them. Some of his paintings were illustrations of what he saw from his wife's tales, others were paintings of Mrs. Rickson in many forms cast in the warmest lights. One of his paintings had her reading under the ray of light shining through the old heavy curtains. The soft glow that surrounded the two of them when they were together was paradise for Mrs. Rickson. She learned to find comfort in the silent moments together.

Despite the blissful days, night would always return. With the darkness came the fear. Mrs. Rickson survived under a duality of warmth and love to cold, daunting fear.

There were nights when Mrs. Rickson would hear whispering outside their bedroom door, but she couldn't make out what they said. She would never stop nearby the basement door. She kept as far away from it as she could. The more Van Rickson painted the happiness he felt, the brighter the house became, but it was always dark in the basement.

Years passed by in this manner, until as it occasionally would, Mrs. Rickson would feel restless and wish to be among the living town they normally observed through thick windows. "Van, it's been a while since we've been anywhere together," Mrs. Rickson said to him one day. "Do you think we can go somewhere else and eat?"

"Your wish is my command," Van Rickson replied. "I believe I know where we can go. I'll phone in a reservation."

"Where are we going?" Mrs. Rickson asked.

Van Rickson grinned, put his finger to his mouth and replied, "It's a secret."

She giggled and kept reading her book while her husband left to make the call. While he was away, she thought she heard a 'thump' downstairs. It made her jump. She took a deep breath and scooted her rocking chair further away from the door. "The house is settling," She repeated her husband's words.

Later that night, Mrs. Rickson was wearing her nicest dress and Van Rickson his finest suit. Mrs. Rickson remembered how hard it was for her before they were married to get Van Rickson to leave his house. It meant a lot to her to know he disliked being in crowded places and yet he would do so because he knew being social made her happy. She spent much of the dinner speaking to her husband, as she always did, about the music she heard or the stories she read. Van Rickson would talk about his paintings and his wife was his most captive audience. It was during this night, however, that she overheard a little bit of gossip.

"It seems like the Rickson hermits decided to come out of hiding," A woman whispered to a man beside her. Mrs. Rickson took an inconspicuous glance around and noticed that they were being watched. Mrs. Rickson shrank in her seat, but when she looked over to Van Rickson, he didn't seem to notice.

On the drive home, as she fidgeted her fingers together, she asked, "Van, do you think that we're hermits?"

"Why would you wonder that?" He asked in return.

"I heard a woman call us the 'Rickson hermits.' Do you think it's true? Have we become so reclusive that we've become some sort of undesirable?"

"It doesn't matter if she's right. We are happy just as we are."

"But hermits, Van? Suppose your reputation is sullied."

Van reached a cold hand out to hers and squeezed it. "It doesn't matter what the world thinks of us. In the end, all we need is each other."

Mrs. Rickson's shoulders relaxed and she smiled. "You're right, dear. I shouldn't be so worried. Since being with you, I've never been so happy."

The days continued, and Mrs. Rickson began to realize that the only person they saw on a regular basis was Mr. Till, Van Rickson's manager, who sold all of the paintings to willing buyers. Before, it didn't bother her. Now she was starting to feel more isolated. She wanted to host parties in their house, which Van Rickson was not interested in. She insisted they go out into the public more, but try as he might, Van Rickson could only stand to be around people so much. "You can go out with your friends and your family," Van Rickson offered. Mrs. Rickson didn't want to admit that in the years they have been married, she became too distant with her friends and her family. Her life centered around him, and she was beginning to feel like it was becoming more of a problem.

A certain macabre film took to the theaters, igniting an interest in darker stories and scarier works of art. Mr. Till came to the Rickson's house, breathless. It just so happened that his client had an entire basement full of dark paintings. Mr. Rickson was thrilled to hear that his lost children would be getting the attention he felt they deserved. Mrs. Rickson, though eager to get them out of the house, couldn't help but feel a pit in her stomach. Until that day, the basement door had been locked. "Please keep the door locked at night at least," She implored.

"I don't understand," Van Rickson replied. "Before we were married, you would come to my house to see me all the time. Now that we are married, you want nothing to do with my old pieces."

"If you recall, I never entered the house when I came to retrieve you," Mrs. Rickson reminded him.

"I thought you admired my art," Van's expression melted lightly.

"I admire your talent and your passion," She admitted. "But I have never felt comfortable around these dark pieces. They seem sinister and hateful."

Van Rickson clutched his chest. "Darling, every single piece I create has a part of me in them. They are part of my soul; they are my life. That is why I call them my children. To hate them would be to hate a part of me."

"I don't hate them, Van. I am afraid of them."

Van put his hands on his wife's shoulders, his eyes square into hers, pleading. "Are you afraid of me?"

She wanted to say 'of course not.' Mrs. Rickson loved her husband more than anything else in this whole world. Despite her conviction, the words wouldn't escape her. She was left to look into the deep, violet eyes of the man that she married, suddenly unsure if they were something beloved or something threatening.

Van Rickson turned away. "I see," He muttered. Mrs. Rickson couldn't think of the words to say in order to explain herself.

To her request, Van Rickson locked the door during the night.

He and Mr. Till looked through them during the day for a few hours, deciding which ones would be featured in a large auction they were planning. They were both expecting a large crowd to come in from this new dark macabre fad. It thrilled Van Rickson that he would be able to share his forgotten children to the world. He coughed.

"Are you feeling well, Mr. Rickson? You've been coughing quite a lot lately," Mr. Till inquired.

"It's nothing serious, I'm sure," Van Rickson replied. He had been moving slower lately, and he seemed more tired, but he was sure it was nothing serious. While before he would smile in Mrs. Rickson's presence, he couldn't even look her way or speak to her. Even in the day, Mrs. Rickson was beginning to feel more alone, and yet, like she was being watched. She would turn quickly in seemingly random directions, but her eyes would always land on one of her husband's paintings. She felt guilt and fear. She felt lonely and paranoid. Mr. Rickson was feeling tired and ill. He imagined and hoped that things would go back to normal if he sold all of the paintings from the basement. He wished for good homes for every piece, any home that wasn't his.

The night of the auction, Mr. Rickson and Mrs. Rickson wore their best for the occasion. Mr. Till had each piece placed and ready to be revealed one by one. There was a huge crowd at the auction, some to get a piece of the famed Van Rickson, others to catch a glimpse of the hermit and his wife. Mrs. Rickson sat in the audience and tried to make conversation, but she was distracted and tired, having been unable to sleep well for the past week, or even perhaps before then. She could feel the tension with every person she spoke with. She could hear their thoughts. 'She's so disconnected,' Mrs. Rickson heard the voices say. 'I'm surprised she's still alive.' Mrs. Rickson's aunt and brother lived out near the coast. She no longer had any friends. She began to feel, without her husband, she was nothing.

"The first piece for tonight," Mr. Till announced. "Is called, 'Death in Silence.' It is oil on canvas and the bidding starts with $10.50." As the room began to ignite with life, Mrs. Rickson stared at the canvas featuring a white-faced being, their mouth covered with the tar-colored tentacle. The white-faced being's eyes were wide, and it grasped at the tentacle and reached for help as it was dragged eternally in the black abyss behind it. Mrs. Rickson felt a chill go up her spine.

"Sold, for $56.42 to number 11," The sound of the gavel hitting wood lurched Mrs. Rickson nearly off her seat. The gruesome painting was taken away to its new owner and another veil-covered piece was put in its place.

She watched as dead-eyed children and twisted mannequins and lurking shadows were placed and sold rapidly among the people. With each piece that was placed, Mrs. Rickson felt more and more that they were looking at her, mocking her. She felt herself tense from the start, breaking out of the moment with each painting only by the coughing of her husband or the banging of the gavel.

They were watching her. She knew that every painting that was unveiled cursed her and mocked her. She couldn't hear the bidding, only the silent whispers that the paintings spoke to her. Because of her, they were banished to the basement. Because of her, the painter was parting with them. Because of her, they were hungry.

Mr. Till presented another veiled canvas. He turned before the audience. "This piece starts at $25. One of our last works up for auction. The latest of the dark paintings created to date; 'The Beast.'"

The veil was ripped from the canvas, and before anything else could be done, Mrs. Rickson stood from her seat and screamed. It alarmed everyone in attendance, especially her husband. He hurried to her side.

"The beast, The Beast!" She wailed. It had a figure black as oil with teeth and fingers sharp as razors. It stood before her, its huge body hovering over her dead father, blood trickling out of his mouth and chest. She re-lived the scene in her mind. There was no doubt. "The Beast," She moaned as she was taken by the arm. "The Beast," She cried as she was dragged out of the building. When she came to, she was greeted with the tired eyes of a distressed beloved.

"Get back!" She pushed him away from her and took a few steps back. "You foul murderer! You horrible fiend!"

"I don't understand," Van Rickson insisted. He tried to take her hand. "Please just take a moment to calm down."

"I will never calm down!" She hollered. "The Beast, you killed my father! You sent The Beast to murder my father!"

"Darling, I don't understand what you're-,"

"Don't you call me darling. To think for all these years, the creature that killed my father was in the basement, and the culprit responsible was sleeping in the same bed! You horrible, monstrous thing!"

Every insult stabbed through Mr. Rickson's body. "It's only a painting, darling. A painting cannot kill anyone."

"No, it's alive. Your precious children are all twisted demons ready to cause harm to everyone," Her eyes widened. "And they're being sold to the whole town."

Mrs. Rickson pushed through the painter. "What are you doing," He cried. She rifled through drawers to find a matchbox and ran into the auction room. Her mind was clouded with only one thought ringing loud and clear; These paintings were demonic creations of dark magic, and they would kill the whole town if she didn't do something. 'The Beast' was being carted away, sold to a gentleman for $104. She sped up to where the paintings waited for their new owners and struck a match. The match was tossed. "Die, demons!" She cried.

"Stop her! Stop that madwoman!" People cried as the oil ignited a few paintings. A crowd of people detained her while others hurried to put out the fire. It charred four or five different paintings, but the rest were saved before any serious damage was done. Mrs. Rickson had to be carried away.

"Mr. Rickson," Authorities came before her. "We're afraid your wife may have lost her mind. We suggest some therapy in the asylum."

"No, I couldn't. I just," Mr. Rickson rung his tie in his hands. He tried to think, but he was haunted by the terror in Mrs. Rickson's eyes as she accused him. "I just need to speak with her. I'm sure I can calm her down."

"I'm afraid that she refuses to see you, sir," One of the officers admitted. "She's convinced that you murdered her father."

Mr. Rickson shook his head. He had sold all of his darker paintings. Things were supposed to get better. He was supposed to live happily with his wife, the love he dedicated his breath to every day. A woman who now detested him, called him a murderer. Perhaps she was sick after all. He clutched his chest and coughed violently. Mr. Till came to his aid.

There was no other choice, Mr. Rickson decided. Soon enough, Mrs. Rickson was arrested and detained in an asylum. The head of the asylum urged Van Rickson to have her remain there until she was cured. She refused to see Mr. Rickson. She wouldn't even call him by name. With the days that followed, Van Rickson rested handsomely on a gratuitous sum of money, which he spent much of it to be sure his wife was given the best care despite his own depleting health. He wanted nothing more than to have his wife well again. He hoped and wished to have everything back to normal. Time after time he came to visit her, and every attempt was met with cold, stabbing silence.

One of the workers at the asylum kept a portrait in his office. It was lightly singed, but it always opened up conversation and he was still very proud of it. The bald-headed face, eyes bulging in terror, was a drastic contrast to the tar-colored tentacles pulling it into the abyss. One night, when all was silent in Mrs. Rickson's cell, black tar began to drip through the cracks of the door. She slowly awoke to the sound of water, but wasn't given time to scream before a long tendril wrapped itself around her nose and mouth.

Early the next morning, Van Rickson was given the news that his wife died during her stay. They were unable to determine the cause, as there was no bruising, no cuts, no evidence. She seemed to have merely stopped breathing in her sleep. They assured him that she passed on peacefully.

The heavy curtains were drawn closed. He turned away all company, including Mr. Till. Van Rickson called on his partner and friend only to bring him food and medicine, as Van Rickson refused to leave his house. Nothing mattered to him anymore. His Angel had forsaken him.

GUILT

Concepta never felt remorse for the things she did. She felt a thrill whenever she robbed someone. A lot of the time, she didn't even want whatever she stole, it was simply the thrill and the satisfaction that she could do it so easily that always appealed to her. The older she got, the easier it was. No one suspected an old woman to rob a neighbor. The blame was pushed to the teenagers in the neighborhood. Many of the houses got wise and strengthened their security, but one day, there was a new family moving in just across the street from her.

Concepta got to work in making a raspberry pie to give them as a welcome to the neighborhood; This was something she did for all the neighbors. While visiting their house after they've unpacked, she could see what sort of things they had.

The raspberry pie was hot and fresh when Concepta left her house. She shuffled over to the other side of the road and rang the doorbell. Concepta's pink skin got goosebumps out in the cold, and she hoped that the family would answer quickly.

A young boy opened the door. He looked up to Concepta with his dark brown eyes and tilted his head. He called out 'mama,' and some other words in a language Concepta herself didn't speak. She waited with a smile when a slender woman wearing a hijab walked up to the door. The woman gave a warm smile and offered the old woman entrance into the home. "I saw you moved in and thought that I would give you a little welcome to the neighborhood," Concepta explained.

"That is very kind of you," The woman replied. She took the pie and set it down on the kitchen counter. "Can I offer you a drink?"

"A glass of water would be nice," Concepta replied. "Where have you moved from?"

"We used to live closer to the coast," The woman answered. "My husband Raahat and I have always wanted to live somewhere quiet for our son to go to school. We are very happy to be here."

"Oh, where are my manners," Concepta straightened up as she proceeded to greet herself. "My name is Concepta. I live right across the street. If there is anything you need, please let me know."

"Thank you," The woman replied. "My name is Aadila. My son's name is Oamra. How long have you lived in this neighborhood," Aadila asked.

"Oh, a very long time," Was Concepta's reply. "I've been here since it was all farmland. A lot of houses were built and people moved here about forty years ago."

"That is impressive. Raahat and I have traveled many times due to his business, although I am hoping that we can stay in this house for a long while. It seems as though the firm has him finally settled down. I may be able to find a teaching job here as well."

"You're a teacher?"

"Yes, it is certainly fortunate that I have work where Oamra and I are home at the same time. With his father always working so many hours, I can't rely on him to be home when Oamra gets home from school."

"With the three of you gone at the same time for so long, it must be difficult for your pets?" Concepta asked.

"Oh, we don't keep pets," Aadila replied.

Concepta grinned. "All the better. They're such a big responsibility and require a lot of spare time to look after." Not to mention, pets made a house more difficult to rob without getting caught. "Well, I should let you rest. You only just moved in, you must be exhausted. I hope you enjoy the pie, and I also hope that I might see you again."

"Yes, of course. Thank you for stopping by. We will tell you how much we like the pie once we taste it. You have been our first visitor, please tell the other neighbors we welcome company."

"I will," Concepta promised. The more visitors, the better. It would make it less obvious when Concepta takes things. Already she had her eye on an expensive silk cloth and a handheld game that belonged to the child. Aadila seemed welcome and trusting, which to Concepta translated as naiive and foolish. It would be easy to take anything she wanted without Aadila realizing it was the sweet old lady across the street.

Concepta cooked dinner at home while she watched the family through the window. The father didn't get home until late that night. Their household was the perfect easy target. Just the thought of the upcoming heist excited her.

She watched the family leave for school and for work a few days more. Once she was sure she understood the pattern and no one was coming back from forgetting anything, she snuck across the street and tested the front door. Of course, it was locked. Concepta expected it. She set down her small lock-picking kit and expertly broke in without any trouble or witness.

The house was decorated in vibrant patterns and knick-knacks. Concepta was on a mission, but although her eyes were on the silk cloth, she found herself catching a glimpse of collectible dolls. No doubt they would be worth a lot, but she would want to come with all of them and make it seem like a break-in from the outside if she was going to get away with such a large haul. For now, things needed to be discreet. She took things small enough to be lost during a move. The more she took, the less time she had, the higher the thrill. Nearly an hour passed, and Concepta locked the door behind her, taking home the haul. She spent the rest of the afternoon admiring the silk cloth and the other small items she grabbed. Hours later, there was a knock at her door, and Concepta put away the items in a room where she kept everything else. She shuffled over to the front door.

"Aadila, it's good to see you again. How are you doing?"

"Not well, honestly," Aadila replied, distressed. "There is a silk cloth and some heirlooms missing from the house. Did you happen to see anything suspicious this morning?"

"Oh, I haven't seen anything, I'm afraid," Concepta lied. "I've been cleaning the house all day. Are you sure it's not things that were lost during the move? I know plenty of things disappear during such a stressful time."

"I wouldn't lose my family's precious heirlooms in a move. I'm certain something happened to them."

"I'm very sorry, dear. I'll be sure to keep an eye out for them if you'd like. Though I'm not sure how much help I can be."

Aadila huffed, putting her hands on her hips. "It's times like this that I wish Alnnawm Alllus was a real thing."

Concepta's eyebrows furrowed, and her head tilted a little. "I'm sorry dear, what was it that you said isn't real?"

"Oh, well I suppose around here it would be called, 'Sleep Thief.' It's an old tale my mother told me about a creature that will come in the night and eat the souls of those with a guilty conscience."

"That sounds gruesome," Concepta commented.

"Well, it is meant to warn thieves and liars. The Alnnawm Alllus would come in the middle of the night and watch you sleep, staring at you with black, bloodshot eyes and tear at your soul with its sharp teeth. It's a very scary tale to make certain that children wouldn't want to risk stealing and lying."

"I've never really been the one that's fond of scary stories," Concepta admitted.

"Oh well it is only a story," Aadila assured her. "Still, it would be nice to have a bit of justice for thievery."

"How can you be so sure it was thievery? Was the door unlocked? Have you seen any sign of break-in?"

Aadila sighed. "You're right, I'm sorry. Perhaps I am getting a little out of hand. It is possible I might have misplaced it. I will go home and check again."

"I'll keep an eye out for you," Concepta told her as she closed the door. She tried to not think about the Sleep Thief. Besides, there was no such thing. Even if there was, Concepta felt no guilt towards what she did. She had been doing it for years, and she'd be doing it years later. What did it matter to her that a few things were missing from people? Most everything got replaced soon enough.

Concepta waited a few weeks for her second heist. This time, she came around the back door which seemed to have accidentally been left unlocked. Concepta grabbed some of the collectible dolls when she heard a car drive up the pavement. She peeked through a window to see that Raahat had come home early from work. She wasn't able to grab all the dolls, but she narrowly got away with four dolls which she really liked. She could hear the man's outrage when he spotted the open back door. "Thief! Thief!" He shouted.

Concepta's mind went to the Sleep Thief.

As she was securing the dolls in her little hoard of stolen things, she could hear Raahat asking the nearby neighbors if they've seen anyone enter his home. Concepta knew no one had, though she overheard one neighbor admitting that the neighborhood had a thief problem. Concepta didn't like that, she'd have to be more careful next time.

She knew exactly what she wanted. She wanted the rest of the collectible dolls that Aadila had displayed in the living room. Concepta had to think about how to do it.

As she slept late at night, she woke up to realize that her chest felt heavier than before. When she opened her eyes in the dead dark, she thought she saw something dash under the bed. She had to remind herself that there was no one in her house. It was only her imagination. Still, she had been waking up in the middle of the night with heavy chest pain quite frequently lately. She hoped that she wasn't getting ill.

There was one last heist Concepta had planned before the new family got wise and raised their security. Concepta wanted to make sure that the rest of the dolls would be hers, but the only way to do that was to finish quickly, and to finish the heist without any large noise.

Concepta had a crazy idea. What if she stole the rest of the dolls in the middle of the night, while the family was asleep? They were expecting for someone to steal them when no one was home, so the neighbors have been paying close attention. However, no one was expecting a heist in the middle of the night. Besides, if the heist was a success, which Concepta was sure it would be, it would prove to her that Concepta was the best thief in the world.

She prepared a night heist. She was meticulous with her plan, making sure everything went right. For some reason, however, as she was getting ready to take the rest of the dolls overnight, she couldn't help but think about the Sleep Thief. Concepta reminded herself that she wasn't guilty of anything. This was a thrill for her, and she didn't care about the items themselves, only the thrill of the steal. It didn't mean that she didn't care about the community or of the new neighbors. She would spend days talking to Aadila over tea or hot chocolate. She watched little Oamra play his games and with his toys. This wasn't against them. She wasn't doing anything wrong.

Once every light was out, Concepta shuffled over beneath the starlight. It was cold, but not yet snowing that winter which Concepta was thrilled about. It would be harder to steal with footprints in the snow. She searched for an unlocked door or window, but then finally found an unlocked window in the kitchen of the house. She crawled through and took a bag with her towards the collectible dolls.

As she started to shuffle all the dolls into the bag, she felt something beneath the couch beside her grab her ankles. She cried out. What grabbed her, she desperately wanted to know. Concepta looked down at the hand that grabbed her and saw behind the couch two white, bulging eyes and rows of sharp teeth. Its large mouth hung open, twisted into a scream. Concepta dropped the bag and tried to pry herself away from the grip of the powerful creature. Concepta shouted and cried out, "Let me go! You monster, let me go!" But the slender, clawed woman only pulled Concepta further under the couch.

Aadila woke up to find her dolls in a garbage bag in the middle of a living room and an open window. She searched everything else, but it seemed as nothing else was compromised. She had the desire to speak to Concepta about it, but the old woman didn't answer the door. Days passed, and neighbors knocked, but there was still no sign of Concepta.

When enough time passed that the town supposed Concepta had passed away in the house or abandoned the building altogether, her house was visited to retrieve her personal belongings. The truth was revealed. Piles of missing items which the neighborhood could identify was scattered all over her house. The entire neighborhood was in shock and supposed that her disappearance was connected with her compulsion. Some believed that she fled because she stole all she wanted to and left satisfied with herself, but they were left to wonder why she left everything behind. Others, like Aadilla, supposed she fled because the guilt finally weighed too heavily on her chest.

THE AUTUMN SPIRIT

In many places of the world, the planet decays a portion of each year. The leaves wither from a vibrant green to different hues of gold and crimson corpses that lay littering the surface. The air is perfumed with scents of hazel and pumpkin, the dew of the morning clings to the atmosphere as the weather chills and darkens. The ground crunches from the weight of small and large critters playing and preparing for the Winter soon arriving. Time itself slows at the presence of autumn, the calm descent of life that preceded it, preparing for the still frozen death that will follow.

Leading the march to this death, it is told, is the Autumn Spirit. Her presence is felt with a shiver of your spine or the aroma of hot chocolate and spice. She is seen with the shower of falling leaves and the presence of glistening dew. Her tattered, auburn garments blanket the ground for their calm, reposeful sleep. Similar to her bitter brother Jack Frost, Autumn changes whatever she touches. Like the Sandman, she lays some to rest. Like Death, flora decays before her. Her pale face and sunken eyes are caught only by the lantern she carries. It beckons with its engaging ochre light, warm among the bite of the breeze.

Her song is the howl of the wind and the chimes of the night. Her presence invites warm baked goods and steaming cups of liquid, presenting itself as solace to the looming stillness. Her ghast presence becomes welcomed by the lanterns glowing through the night and the hearth warming the burrows and caves of familiar creatures gathering for ardor to last them the chiller seasons to follow. Autumn is the season of closeness and connection. Hold the loved ones tight as Autumn glides past your door. Bundle yourself against the cold and take in the fragrance of damp earth and cinnamon. Autumn Leaves fall and blankets your world tonight.

THE WORLD BENEATH OURS

You may believe I am crazy, and you may be right. But I have seen the world that hides behind ours. I have seen the stitches on the fabric of our reality. I am being taken away, cousin, but I plead only that you read what I have to say and consider what I may have seen. This world is tied together with a fine thread of complacency. I have heard theory become fact by the random test and false numbers of one man's claim to discovery. I have seen fiction become life by the blind belief of some desperate desires breathed immortal for the end goal of omnipotence. Cousin, every living being that we have encountered lives in a falsehood that has been fashioned to their ideal image. We are bound together only by the similarities we have shared. Do I sound mad? Perhaps that is why I am being taken to a house designed for the mad. Nevertheless, endure cousin, for I have much to share with you.

It was on my way to shop when I first witnessed it; the fabric of my earth rippled and I beheld a sinister sight. As I drove on, I came right toward it. I was advancing toward a plump man with a bowler hat and cane. However, as I came closer, I had discovered that what I saw was not what was seen, and that the thing I had mistaken as a plump man was an ordinary bush. Odd, I mused, for I have never seen such a clear view morph into a vastly different thing so quickly. I was perplexed, cousin, but like all rational beings I had considered it an error on my own cognition and continued driving to the market. This was only the beginning, cousin.

My home is a sacred place, sedentary. As you are well aware, I enjoy everything in its rightful place. I can close my eyes and go about my normal domestic routine. As I was washing my dishes after supper, I caught a glimpse of something reflected off the window. Behind me, there was a tall, hunched being with an outstretched hand, reaching for me. I spun around to catch the intruder, clutching a kitchen knife in my fist to face my foe. To my astonishment, the man in question was my raincoat draped over the vacuum. It had been in the same spot for years, but I had never made that mistake before.

My reality was unraveling, cousin. I was seeing things that I had never seen before. Even still I did the best I could to cling to the garments of the universe I had created around me. I went to an optometrist and told her about my situation. She referred me to a neurologist, who in turn could find nothing wrong. It was a very expensive goose chase.

There was nowhere else to turn for me. I, like any rational creation, believed science to give me all the answers. Becoming obsessed with the situation, I decided to study up on the most basic element of all of mankind's achievements which, to no surprise, is philosophy. Cousin, in case you are not aware, before there was schooling, there was philosophy. It is the mother of both science and religion. It is like the infinite space where all the elements meet together to create the matter that we are familiar with. It is the mysterious blackness rich in potential where stars and planets and life are slowly formed. It is, in all its realities, using all the information known to you regardless of bias in order to make sense of each piece and create an idea.

This was the void in which I floated, gathering every bit of information I could remember learning. I had remembered stories of other people who have experienced strange phenomenon as I recently had. There are stories of demons and spirits and extraterrestrial creatures as well as fairies and magical things. I have lately wondered why so many people discredit such things as fiction. Undoubtedly, many occurrences can be proven to be a hoax, but there are several that never had been explained. Could some believe that if some were false, then all must be? Could they maybe unconsciously fear that their made-up mind becomes compromised by the inclusion of new information? Perhaps both are true. We shouldn't be so afraid of the unknown. I believe there will be less to fear if we learned how to embrace it.

But then again, perhaps the will to accept and decline information is partly why we have so many points of view. I had caught myself, cousin. I had begun to wonder if, for every individual's quest for 'Truth,' perhaps there is none. A flower doesn't bloom knowing why it exists. A dog does not question why good and bad things happen to it. Every one of us are collecting small portions of data, and the sooner we close our minds the sooner we will be proven wrong. Time and space and our existence is always advancing and changing, but it is frightful for most to humor the possibility that nothing is certain and everything can be altered. So in order to keep our sanity and to not keep delving on an amorphous concept of what is perception and what is true facts, we settle on the unstable ground hoping that it doesn't cave in before us, despite floating on plates on top of a fluid core. Consider that, cousin. We are floating on a core of lava. We live with the illusion of certainty and solidarity in order to prevent... Well, in order to prevent becoming as I am now.

But cousin, it is important to remember, even if from the farthest reaches of your coherent mind, that anything can change at any moment. It is important to not try and remain solid when everything else is fluid. I have realized that a solid mind in a fluid world sinks unless you are content with having a mind that is flat or hollow. The only way to become part of the world is to also become fluid, so that is what I did.

We base our knowledge based on the things we can perceive. If I touch fur, see large ears and a twitchy nose, I will call it a rabbit, or at the very least a rodent. Our categories and our circles and boxes that we create in order to understand the world are mostly based off of the things we learn based on what we've perceived. Take, for example, the bush I confused as a man with a bowler hat. Was it a bush the whole time, or was it, for that moment, a man in a bowler hat as I had perceived it? For that second, the man in the bowler hat existed. I saw them, I perceived them, I acknowledged his existence. Now he exists in your mind too, doesn't he cousin? Suppose I told you that I met a man in a bowler hat, omitting the fact that he later became a bush. To you, the man would exist, wouldn't he? You would be aware that I had witnessed a portly man wearing a bowler hat and he would exist as a human being to you.

Suppose I told you about the tall man reaching for me in my house. You would be alarmed perhaps about how a tall man entered my house. You may wonder what became of the tall man. He would exist in the moment you interrogate me. But what would happen if what became of him was that he became my rain coat hung over a vacuum? Would the man then disappear completely, or would his image you created for him remain in your mind? He may not be here for others to experience, but he does now exist with you. Perhaps in order to be real, a number of people would have to perceive it.

We have creatures and beings that are claimed to have been visited by a number of people. There are entire populations of individuals who have stories of strange creature sightings, alternate dimensions and pattern-like situations. Some even have video, audio or photographic evidence to prove they are in existence, so why are they discredited then? Certainly, there are false claims and altered audio, but that is not the case for everything. In those cases, those things do not only exist but they do so widely among many people. I wonder, cousin, what came first? Imagination or unexplained occurrences? Were these strange scenarios born from imagination, or vice-versa? It may not seem so curious to someone who has not witnessed the stranger things, but a baffling sum of people know and remember what happens when the ground gives way from under them. It's a type of fear mixed with invigoration that jolts me awake at night.

I keep seeing them now, cousin. I see the world beneath the magma core and the moving plates. I see the shadows behind the objects and the presence behind the void. I am no longer afraid of the unknown, because I am no longer afraid of an open mind. Knowledge and criticism and fact and fiction all flow through me with no filter and I take it all into consideration. I've seen the tendrils of the darker creatures and the wings of the ones surrounded by light. I see them everywhere, and I speak to them, and they react to me. I do not live in your world anymore, cousin, and I do miss you. I looked to my wall and I swear I saw you, sitting there with a book in your hand. Were you skimming the words as you normally do? Were you reading the words at all? Cousin, although we may have never met, I can see you. An open mind is a wonderful thing. I wonder if you understand how radiant you look when focusing so intently.

Although I do enjoy being able to see the other world, cousin, I do sometimes miss the old place. You exist there, in that place. Even if the surface is uncertain, I do sometimes miss the illusion that it was, but I know too much now to go back to that. I truly hope that you will venture enough to visit me here, cousin. There are so many things I want to show you.

MYSTERIOUS PLACES

Have you ever been somewhere so amazing that you never wanted to leave? Was that place ever somewhere that didn't really exist? I remember that place.

It was freaky at first, I used to not remember my dreams when I went to sleep. When I found myself in this forest with no way out, I started to panic. I was relieved when I woke up, but it stuck with me even throughout the day. I couldn't stop thinking about it. I told my buddy Wes which I immediately regretted when he chuckled.

"Dude, you were scared of a forest in your dream? It doesn't seem like something to be creeped out by," Wes replied.

"Yeah, but I never remember my dreams and then all of a sudden I'm in this forest with no escape," I explained.

"Will, dude, if you wanna hear about scary dreams then I can tell you a ton of them. Once I dreamed that you, me and Zach were in this building and I think we were renting a moving truck for some reason, but then the place caught fire and we died. Dying is freakier than some forest."

"Yeah, whatever man. I dunno, it was just weird." I wanted Wes to understand somehow that it was abnormal. Regardless, I dropped the subject. I considered telling Zach about it later since Zach and I were roommates and he was pretty open to listening, but he had enough to deal with what with his ex messing with him. Besides, Wes was right, it was just a dream and it wasn't that horrifying in retrospect.

I forgot about it for a while. I was trying to work for this couple who just started a business, but they had no idea what they were doing. I gave the restaurant maybe six months before it went under. They were nice people, but they really needed some more direction if they were gonna start their own food company. The free food was a decent perk, though. I ended up quitting the job, it was painful to see them floundering and they were having trouble paying me, anyway.

The night after I quit, I found myself in the forest again. I was wandering around, paying little attention to the area around me. I decided to run in one direction until I could see something familiar. I heard voices of my parents, so I ran that way. From the other way, I heard Wes and Zack calling around for me. I hesitated before I started running towards them instead. I tried to cry out to them, but my voice was too soft. I tried to shout louder, and I finally did, but to no satisfaction. The forest became still. I strained to listen for any voices, but there wasn't anything at all. I didn't hear the wind through the trees, no critters running around, not even my own breathing. The forest was so silent that I began to feel scared again. Was there nothing here?

I turned around, but froze. There was a deer in the distance. It wasn't making any noise, but I felt relief in seeing another living creature. As it walked forward, sniffing the ground, I became aware of some disturbing differences to any normal deer. First of all, the deer was huge. It was more the size of a moose, but probably even a little bigger than that. I've never seen a moose before, but I imagined its back would be higher than me. This thing had to be at least ten feet tall without the antlers. The antlers, however, stretched out high and split into a lot of different places, twisting into spirals at the end.

When the creature turned its head to look around, I flinched. The deer had four eyes. Two on each side, one above the other. The part that made me flinch though was the mouth. It had white, sharp scissor-like teeth. The nose wasn't at the end of the muzzle, it was almost between the lower set of eyes. The mouth, instead of going left to right, split the muzzle down the middle starting a little bit down the nose. Its muzzle stretched apart and I was able to see its lips curl away from the teeth as it yawned. Curiously, my heart didn't race. My body didn't tense. I did, however, feel my body tingling everywhere. It was like my skin wanted to separate from my body, or like hundreds of worms were digging through my body just beneath the surface. The thing turned its head to look right at me.

When my eyes opened, my body was still tingling, but I now had the freedom to rub my arms and legs and shake the feeling away. "What the hell was that?" I said to myself. I was first alarmed that my clock was blaring nearly noon, but settled down when I remembered that I quit my job. I felt immediately tired thinking I'll have to start looking for another job, but refrained from going back to sleep with the deer still fresh in my mind. I wanted to tell Wes, but he'd probably be a jerk about it again. I decided to tell Zack once he got back from work.

I spent the day trying to work up the energy to look for another job but ended up just watching videos on the internet. I somehow found myself at a funny animal video when Zach barreled through the door. "Hey man," I started. He tossed his keys on the counter and offered a light mumble of recognition before pulling out his phone and going into his room.

Maybe telling him about a weird dream I had wasn't the best thing for now. I left him alone to shower and argue with his ex while I kept watching videos and browsing the internet. Eventually I got frustrated with myself doing nothing to the point where I had a list of places written down that were looking for employees. Satisfied, I went to bed.

I was nervous for a few nights, thinking that I was going to dream about the forest again, but days went by really quickly and I didn't remember a single dream. I was beginning to think everything was back to normal. Wes, Zach and I decided to go to a Monster Truck rally one night. It had been forever since I've been to one. Wes drove up to us on his new motorcycle to show it off. "Check it out," He grinned. "Isn't she awesome?"

"Yeah, man," Zach crossed his arms with a smirk. "It's almost as awesome as my bike."

"Whatever Zach, your piece of junk needs a lot of work."

"Well how about we have a race sometime and then we'll see which one needs work," Zach replied. He looked my way, "Will, you can be the flag." Both of them laughed.

"Shut up, Zach," I mumbled. They liked to give me a hard time ever since I had my license revoked. I got pulled over and hit with a DUI, and it would be another four months before I was allowed to get a new one. On top of that, I didn't have a stable job so I not only didn't have money for a bike, but if I didn't find some way to make money soon I'd be in debt with Zach for rent. I felt guilty about how much of a deadbeat I was. Zach was pretty much supporting the both of us. I had no car, no license, no job, I hardly cleaned, I didn't cook, I just retreated into my room and spent the day bingeing on movies and browsing the internet. I couldn't even provide emotional support. I was horrible at giving advice or paying attention or really caring much for anyone's problems. Before I was able to justify all my faults because at least I was paying rent. The severity of needing to find work soon made my body tense.

We went inside the arena where the rally would be taking place. Wes bought me some food which I told him I'd pay him back, but I was sure he wasn't holding his breath. I planned to make good on my debts eventually. We got into the rally and found our seats. Zach had earplugs because he couldn't handle the sound and didn't want to go deaf. Wes and I gave him a lot of shit for it. The motorcycle racing was by far the most interesting of the opening acts. One of the guys messed up in midair and hit his head on the handle. He let go of the motorcycle which hit the hay circling the course and he fell to the ground unconscious. They had to get a stretcher to take the guy to the hospital. A lot of people were hoping that he'd be okay. There was a bit of intermission to get everyone back in the excitement of monster trucks. Some more people did tricks on motorbikes. Two cars dressed up like dragons fought it out with fire coming out of their mouths.

Then there came the main event. The announcer shouted over the crowd and the sound of revving engines, introducing the trucks that were going to perform. Wes knew about most of the guys, he kept up with the monster truck names and the drivers. He kept telling me a little bit about each driver that came out, like I cared. I just wanted to see some cars get crushed.

"But hold on," The announcer shouted as the trucks lined up. "We have a newbie on the race today! Already a crowd favorite, she tears apart the smaller trucks like paper! She gives even the biggest drivers a run for their money. Give it up for Diana Gracey and the Crushing Cannibal!"

The final truck entered the ring. I felt myself raising from my seat and grabbing Zach and Wes's shoulders. "It's the thing," I cried before I completely registered what was going on.

Painted on each side of the truck was the deer from my dream. It was black with glowing white eyes, staring at me. It was vaguer than when I saw it, but the silhouette was no mistake. I found myself having a hard time breathing.

"The hell is wrong with you, Will?!" Zach shouted at me. Wes, who must have heard me despite the crowd, chimed in. "What 'thing?' Sit your ass down, you're being an idiot."

"The thing from the dream," I tried to clarify as I sat between them again. I immediately regretted it. Wes and Zach both looked at me like I had gone insane. I think I heard Zach say 'what dream' but it was drowned in cheers and revving engines. My friends turned to focus on the race while I had a tunnel vision on the decal on the Crushing Cannibal. Could the driver know what the deer was? Did she have the same dream? On the other hand, could it maybe be that I've seen this picture somewhere before and just dreamed it up later? I really wanted to know, but I didn't want to seem like a creep to anyone. Throughout the whole show, I struggled with what was stronger, my curiosity over the decal or my fear of humiliation?

After the show, the racers met everyone in the lobby to give out autographs and merchandise. I took a brochure of the race and stood in line to speak with Diana, to the annoyance of my friends. I watched her talk to everyone as they came up to her. It was a relief to see that she seemed really nice. She even posed for a few pictures without any hesitation. I felt less nervous approaching her, but I was still worried that she would think I was a complete nutcase.

"Will you sign this?" I asked her. After a second, I added a quick, "Please?"

"Yeah, absolutely!" She agreed. "Did you like the show?"

"I, uh, yeah, it was good," I shrugged. "Um, actually, I have a question about your truck."

"Sure, I'm always up for answering questions."

"I kinda was wondering about the decal," I blurted. "Is it like, maybe inspired by anything, or..." I trailed off, gesturing awkwardly with my hands. She looked at me with a blank face, like she didn't understand the question. In hindsight, I think she was assuming the question would be about the mechanics so I must have thrown her off.

"Oh, you mean what's the inspiration behind the Crushing Cannibal? Actually, I don't really know. I got the decal commissioned from this guy and he did a really great job. It looked familiar almost, but I guess it's because it looks so much like a deer."

"So, you don't know where it came from? It's just a deer someone drew?"

"Well no, I commissioned a creature that looked innocent but is a little terrifying and the guy drew this. It wasn't meant to look like a deer specifically, but I guess that's the innocent part I asked for. I love how graceful it looks, but the eyes and teeth and the weird mouth makes it surreal."

"So, you didn't, like, dream it up or anything?"

Diana raised an eyebrow. I felt like maybe I should have stopped while I was ahead. "No, I don't ever remember my dreams. Seems like a kind of creepy thing to dream up though, huh?" She offered.

I knew she was just trying to be polite and not make me feel like a total idiot, but I was so flustered that I just wanted to get out of the situation. "Well, thanks," I replied before turning to leave. I almost forgot to grab the pamphlet I asked her to sign.

"If it helps," She called out to me. "The guy I commissioned it from has an account online. His username is Dreamscape3636."

My face was hot, but through the embarrassment I tried my best to remember that username. At the very least, I could maybe go through his archive. Wes was laughing at me, but Zach didn't say anything. I tried to keep from looking at them.

Once we got home, Zach blocked me from going to my room. "Dude, what was up with you tonight?"

"Huh?" I looked up at him. We both knew I was acting like a total weirdo, but I didn't want to confess to anything. I didn't want him to act like Wes did. "Nothing dude, why?"

"First it was the grabbing mine and Wes's arms and freaking out, then you just had to talk to the truck driver, and the whole way home you were just completely vacant. Will, what's up with you?"

I sighed. He just had to go and spell it all out. I had to tell him something, and I wasn't quick enough to think up a good lie. "Alright. Well, I had a dream and the decal on the truck just looked like something from the dream, okay? But it turned out to be nothing."

"You had a dream that had a creature look like that?" Zack raised an eyebrow.

"Yeah, but it doesn't matter. I think I maybe just didn't remember seeing a picture of the thing online or something and I dreamed about it. It was just strange because I usually don't remember my dreams but every time I've remembered a dream so far it's been in this damn wooded area and it's freaking me out a little bit. Even though I know it's stupid to get scared about dreams, I just can't help it. But it's really nothing, it's fine."

"Will, you know my sister knows about weird dreams and stuff. You want me to contact her or whatever? I mean, if it'll calm you down."

"No," I looked away. I didn't want everyone to know I've been losing my mind over two dreams. "I haven't had the dream in like, a week. I'm sure it's fine. Thanks, though."

"Yeah, no problem," Zach replied, hesitant. He passed me to get to his room and get ready for bed. I was left in my room to my thoughts, wondering if the deer was really something I saw before or if there was something else to it. I kept trying to tell myself to let it go, but something kept me connected to it.

"Dreamscape3636," I recalled. I sat up and pulled out my laptop. I had to know. Of course, the internet was slow. It always seemed to be the slowest when I needed the internet most. It certainly wasn't this slow when I was browsing. I searched the name for images, and to my relief there were results. There was a blog and an 'About' page for Dreamscape3636. "This better not get me malware," I muttered.

I read the 'About' page and found out very little. The guy's real name was Diego Francisco. He's been doing art for years, and he listed a bunch of inspiration artists with creepy backstories like Van Rickson and Rita McGrary. I saw the decal he drew for the monster truck driver and he had up this piece with a hunched-over humanoid creature with a long neck and a needle in its hand, but everything else required a subscription to the website to see. I considered it, then remembered I had no job and no money. I sighed, frustrated. This looked like another dead-end. I put the laptop away, then went to bed. I spent what felt an hour staring at the ceiling. Eventually, I drifted asleep.

I was running through the forest, trying to get away. Everything looked the same. I couldn't find anything to mark my spot. At one point, I couldn't run anymore, despite not feeling out of breath, and hid myself behind a tree. While I sat there, I noticed that there was a cave nearby. Curious, I walked towards it. I felt the mouth of the cave. It was cold, rough and bumpy. A dark blue crystal covered the entire mouth. I wandered in a little closer. It felt claustrophobic, and for a moment, I was trying to convince myself to leave. Once I was completely inside, however, I was entranced by the glistening sparks of white, yellow, blue and red among a space that was otherwise completely black. For a time, it felt as though I was standing in the middle of space looking on to the countless galaxies beyond. Before I felt claustrophobic, but now I felt so small. What meaning was there to my life?

The dark galaxy faded and morphed into my room's ceiling. I stared at it for a small time. Weird, for the first time I didn't wake up scared of the forest. Instead, I felt almost motivated. I thought about the galaxy cave. It stuck with me while I filled out application after application. I had thirteen done by the time I realized I hadn't eaten all day. Zach was due to return from work soon, so I figured, why not cook some dinner and have some leftovers for him?

It wasn't fancy; I just popped a lasagna in the oven and threw some bagged veggie mix into the microwave. Even so, I felt accomplished. Zach came in just as I was serving myself up a plate. "Hey Zach, I made dinner You're welcome to it."

Zach faltered a little and set his keys down. His eyes were wide. "Whoa, Will, are you feeling alright?"

"Shut up and eat, asshole," I replied. "I just felt like cooking, okay?"

"You've never cooked in the entire time I've known you. Who are you and what have you done to Will?"

"Are you going to eat it or not? It's just shit I threw together, it's no big deal." Regardless, Zach seemed a little bugged about it. I didn't see anything wrong with it, I just wanted to celebrate having accomplished a bunch and I didn't have money to order pizza so lasagna was the next best thing. Whatever, I thought, Zach could think what he wanted.

Zach got a plate for himself. He complimented the food, as though I did more than just heat it up. Still, it was appreciated. I could see he wanted to talk to me about something. I figured it was about his ex, but it never came up. Instead we talked about movies we liked and stuff we both wanted to do once we were in a better place. I didn't tell him, but I was relieved to talk with him. Even though we were both so lonely, for that night, we were together.

A couple days passed and I still hadn't heard anything from the places I applied to. Finding a job was always so long and grueling, it took me four months to find work at the failing restaurant and I had to find that through a friend. I was starting to get nervous about the whole situation. What if no one hired me? Was all that work before for nothing?

In the nights where I dreamed, I entered the forest with a less panicked feeling. I started to take in the trees and the plants around me. There were a lot of plants that I didn't recognize, some that I didn't think could even exist in reality. One night, as I continued to wander around the alien terrain which was slowly becoming more like home, I heard something go 'Meep.'

It was faint, but abrupt enough for me to take notice and look around. I heard it again. It sounded almost like a kitten, the kind that would squeak instead of meow. I wandered near a clearing and before me, in a ray of spotlight, was a long-tailed rabbit with blue fur. It 'meeped' again, its entire body jumping at the act. It scurried around, sniffing the ground before uprooting what looked like a radish except it was gray and twice as large. I watched it nibble on the vegetable while other 'meep' sounds surrounded us. Other little cat-rabbits came out to look for gray radishes. Some had yellow fur, others were red, and there were some light green ones as well. Their pastel coloring reminded me of spring. Some cuddled against each other, others jumped on each other and tugged their long ears. Some batted at others' tails. They looked so furry, I wanted to pet one. I began to bend down when I spotted something peeking from the other side of the clearing.

Its large antlers camouflaged with the swirly branches of the trees, and its tan coat kept its large body inconspicuous, but I could see four bright green eyes on a lowered head. I froze.

The deer was so swift, I didn't even notice it moved until the cat-rabbits fired up a commotion of 'meeps' and began to scatter. One of the cat-rabbits squealed. I turned my attention to the little blue one I saw first, thrashing as it was picked up by the deer. The mouth covered most of its tiny, furry body, and then to my horror, I saw the cat-rabbit twist and go limp after the deer's maw snapped closer together with a loud 'crunch!'

I shot up from bed, panting. I turned to the clock that read 3PM. I really had to start correcting my sleep schedule. I tried to calm down my heart with a glass of water and some macaroni and cheese. Zach caught me in the dining room.

"Dude, you've been asleep all day. Are you sick?"

"Maybe," I lied.

"Well, just don't give it to me. I can't miss any work right now."

I felt a twinge of guilt. I was really hoping to have a new job by now. "Yeah, got it. I don't think I'm contagious."

"Yeah, alright," Zach fell silent for a minute before he spoke again. "Hey, Will? Uh, so I used to look after this kid, right? He was a pretty cool kid, but he didn't talk to anyone when he was upset and... Well, just... If you need to talk to someone, just keep me in mind, okay?"

I looked over to him, brows furrowed. This story of Zach's past babysitting career felt like it came out of nowhere, but I'd be lying if I pretended that I didn't appreciate it. I smirked and nodded his way. "Yeah. Thanks," I told him.

He nodded and stood there a couple seconds before he left to go to his room. It occurred to me that I hadn't asked how he was doing lately, and I didn't get any update on what was going on with his ex. I was too upset to go ask though, and I was too embarrassed to admit that I was upset about a fictional blue rabbit to tell Zach about it.

I was only awake enough to eat and watch videos online for a couple hours before I felt overwhelmingly tired again. I figured that if I went to sleep now, I could wake up earlier and I could get my sleep schedule back on track. I set my alarm for 10am, that was more than twelve hours of sleep. The plan was to wake up before then, but I had the alarm set anyway. I was nervous about dreaming about the deer again, but I couldn't bear to stay awake, either.

I was running again, but this time I seemed to recognize the directions I was going. The strange plants and the caves became familiar. I heard the beating of hooves behind me, but I couldn't hear my own footsteps. I couldn't hear my breathing. All I could do was keep running despite the hoof-prints gaining on me.

I arrived at a part of the forest I've never seen before. The reason I knew it was new was because it had trees I remembered existing in the real world. This part of the forest looked normal. The hoof-beats no longer pounded behind me. I started to walk, wondering if there could be a path or something to help me find my way back. I noticed a soft, white glow in the distance. I thought it might be the moon, so I hurried towards it. To my astonishment, there was no moon. On a large tree alone in a clearing, there was a woman's face with long white hair. Her eyes were closed and her mouth was gaping open, as though she were in the middle of a yawn. Her hair glistened and flowed like individual strands of cobwebs. I stared at the being, mortified and curious. Besides the deer, there had been nothing to try to hurt me before. But I was certainly intimidated by the decapitated glowing woman head.

This was the first time I encountered something remotely human. Everything felt as though it was standing still, waiting for me to do something. "Can you tell me how to get home?" I asked her.

I didn't know what sort of reaction I was expecting. Her stillness was haunting. After a moment of silence, I noticed that her silver hair started to grow. It did so slowly at first, but then it started flowing to the ground and the fine strands rushed like a stream deeper into the forest. I watched it disappear into the thick leaves and bushes. I was almost afraid to turn back around to look at the woman's face, but was relieved when I saw she was still exactly where she was the whole time. Did I need to follow the hair? It was bizarre, but so was everything else around here. Without any more hesitation, I began walking toward the direction of the hair.

Small orbs of light surrounded my path, illuminating it. No matter how thick the forest got, I could always see it. Somehow, I knew that if I deviated from the path, I would never find it again. It made me tense. The hair looked so soft and silky, but I was too afraid to touch it. I just kept following it, watching as the landscape around me changed from familiar back to the alien world I seemed to have grown accustomed to.

I traveled for entire minutes without anything interesting happening, but after a while, I heard the sound of water. I picked up the pace, rushing over to where I could hear it. I came across a stream small enough to jump over it. The water was so clear and inviting. I could see little fish swimming against the current and then giving up, being swept away before swimming back to the same spot and trying to rush against the current again. Further down, there were frogs, except these frogs were scaly and had a more violet color. They croaked and hopped around like any ordinary frog. I saw my first bird by the stream as well. It had vibrant pastel colors and a light orange glow at the end of each tail feather. Come to think of it, many creatures and plants had some luminescent quality.

I marveled at the small creatures around me for a little bit. I never thought about looking at the nature at home as often as I did here. After a while though, I remembered my quest to get out of the forest. While passing through the stream, I was suddenly aware of how cool and wet the water was. The sudden sensation of feeling took my attention. I wondered how long I've been sleeping. My alarm hadn't gone up yet, so everything must be fine at home. I watched as slowly, more and more small creatures emerged from hiding. Were they always around in my previous dreams and I just wasn't paying attention?

My attention was turned to the top of the trees. I hadn't noticed before, but there were large spider webs on the trees. I focused my attention and noticed that, camouflaged within the trees were spiders the size of cats with bristling cameo fur. Calico spiders? Wes would be terrified of something like that, but I was never really scared of bugs. I wondered if the spiders could be trained like pets. I could train one to make a hammock for me while I rest under the shade of these trees. I caught myself wondering things as though I planned to stay. What was I thinking? I was leaving. I wasn't about to stay here.

'Focus, Will,' I told myself. I had to keep reminding myself that the goal was ahead of me. I started to jog a little so that there would be less time between me and wherever the hair ended. Once I got a few yards ahead, I noticed an obstacle staring at me in the distance with its glowing green eyes. I froze. The deer was looking right at me. I wanted to run, but I couldn't leave the path. I thought about running back the other way, but my body wouldn't turn around. I just had to watch in terror as the deer came closer to me. It was so large that it could trample me with no trouble. My hands were shaking, and I swallowed. I remained perfectly still. Would it bite me in half like it did the poor blue cat-rabbit?

The deer lowered its head and sniffed me. It shook its head, stared at me, then took a step back. I watched it slowly bow its head. Afraid and unsure of what to do, I thought that it was usually polite to bow in return, so that's what I did.

Once I had bowed my waist, the deer pushed its nose against my shoulder. I raised my hands to keep from falling back, and I placed my hand on its muzzle. It pressed against my hand. It closed its eyes and nuzzled against me. Did it want me to pet it?

My hand almost started moving on its own. I started cradling the large head, petting its head between the horns and its ears and its nose. The deer was so affectionate, I started to chuckle. I was afraid of this thing? It was like a big dog, just craving attention. "If I'd have known you were this cool to begin with, I probably wouldn't have been running in the first place."

The deer tilted its head. I stopped petting it and started walking my path again. "Sorry buddy, I have to go home."

The deer didn't follow me. It just watched as I kept going on my path through the forest. Every so often I would look back and the deer would always be in the distance, hesitantly following like a stray pet. At one point, I felt so bad that I couldn't look back anymore. This place was so full of so many cool plants and animals, and I didn't seem to ever be in any danger. Honestly, it was like heaven.

I started to hear voices, and honestly, I didn't believe it at first. It was so ethereal for me. But when I heard my name, I knew that I was finally close. I started running towards the bright light.

Just outside the clearing that bridged my dream and the real world, I witnessed a scene with me in a hospital room. Wes and Zach were both there along with my older brother, my parents and my aunt. They were gathered around me, who lay in a hospital bed with a respirator. I put my hand to my mouth. I could feel it there.

"He just didn't wake up," Zach's voice trembled. "His alarm went off but he never woke up. He didn't wake up all day, or that night, or the morning after... I should have called sooner."

"You've done everything you could," My aunt assured him. "I just wish the doctors could tell us what's wrong with him."

Everything got darker. I looked down to see the stream of hair dull and fade away. This was the place where I had to choose. I didn't know how I knew, but one way or the other, my choice would be permanent.

The decision should have been easy. All I would have to do is go through this clearing and into my body, then I would wake up and be free from the woods forever. But then I started thinking about the woods. I thought about the beautiful places I've been and the creatures I've seen. I've felt this feeling of peace throughout most of the journey. For the first time, I had to think of what I was going back to. The world was full of hate and anger and boredom. I was unemployed without anyone to love romantically and no future. I didn't have any real hobbies, I owed a ton of money, and I didn't have any passion to do anything to impact the world.

On the other hand, there was my family and the people I cared about. I didn't want them to be upset, and I knew that they'd miss me. I wanted to pay back Wes and Zach. I wanted to fall in love and see my family and be part of the chaos of the world.

But once I leave here, I could never go back. I'll lose the forest forever. I'll be unhappy all the time and it would just worry my family even more. Heck, I might even become crazy after the things I've seen here. And after everything was said and done, wouldn't my family want me to be happy?

I was happy here in this forest. Finally, I could admit it. I wanted to stay here with the deer and the cat-rabbits and the nature. Maybe there were other people here, too. There was so much left to explore. In the end, I had to decide. Would I rather try to help fix an old world, or discover a new one?

I turned away from reality. I could see in the distance, the deer waited for me. I walked over to her. I didn't hear my footprints or any breathing, only hoof-beats, calm and rhythmic like the beat of a fading heart.

Have you ever thought about your childhood home? The place where you learned and grew and moved on from? Sometimes I think back and miss that place, but I'm much happier here where I am. Despite my newfound happiness, I remember that old place. I'll never forget it.

PRINCETON'S JOURNAL: MIRROR BRIDE

Dear Rory,

I don't think I feel very safe taking Sandra out on these ghost hunts anymore. Granted, neither of us felt completely okay with it in the first place, but now I am really starting to worry that this could have a bad effect on her. This latest case had me really worried. I'll start from the beginning and see what you think.

It started as normal, just a family with an old house that says it's haunted and they want me to see if I can find anything. The second I arrived, I noticed that there was a single small window in the attic. I had a gut feeling about that window, and you know how things are with my gut-feelings. Still, I decided to follow your advice and not run to any conclusions right away. Sandra, of course, couldn't wait to get into the house. She loves going on these hunts with me more than anything. I thanked the couple and told them to return in a few days and hopefully by then I would have answers.

"I didn't know you had a daughter," The husband told me. "Please be really careful, out of all the people in our family, our youngest daughter seems to be the one that's affected the most."

"Thank you for telling me that," I replied. "Before you leave, tell me exactly what sort of things you've noticed about the house."

"Well it started with the kids talking about seeing this woman at the corner of their eye. She wears a wedding dress. Then our youngest daughter started sleepwalking and more than once she would go to the bathroom, look into the mirror and say some very... Disturbing things."

"Understood, sleepwalking, sightings of the same woman... It sounds like a poltergeist. Certainly, one of the more dangerous spirit types to date. She must be vengeful."

"You've got that right," The husband responded. "My wife heard a screaming and then our bedroom window shattered and some of the shards cut her legs and feet. That was the last straw, it's why we decided to call you. I can't have my wife and children in danger."

"Windows, mirrors... I'm beginning to see a pattern already. Does this house have any history?"

"I'm not sure. I didn't think to check."

"That'll be my first step then. Do you have internet access?"

"Of course," The man gave me the wifi password. I thanked him and let him join his family. I wasn't so sure the screaming was the spirit. So far as you and I have gathered, brother, spirits tend to prefer darkness and silence. However, we have to agree that poltergeists always seemed to deviate from the norm. They possess people like some stronger demons, but they can also affect objects like trinkets can and they're not always easy to pinpoint. No easy fix here, and now I had Sandra to worry about. I thought about sending her to you, but the plane ticket would be worth the whole amount I was getting for this gig.

"Sandra, stay close to me," I called out to her.

"'Kay," She replied and sat with me at the kitchen table. She kept looking around trying to find the spirit. Eventually she gave up and started reading a book. I went through the computer to try and see something about this town or this house. There wasn't a whole lot to go on, but I eventually found a published book with some local urban legends of the area. There were a bunch of them, but of course there were always a ton no matter where you went. There wasn't anything about this house in particular, but there was a story that sounded very similar to our poltergeist.

There was a murder. A husband and wife lived somewhere quite a way from here almost 200 years ago, but the wife was killed during their honeymoon and the husband disappeared with all her money and took the ring he gave her for the wedding. The man's name was Derek Wan and his wife's name was Kimberly Young. "Kimberly, huh," I muttered. As I did, I saw my reflection on the computer screen flip to a ghastly sunken-eyed woman with a gaping mouth and matted hair.

"Ho!" I hollered and slammed the computer closed. It startled Sandra who looked up from her book. It took a second to steady my heart, but I remembered that even though I can't see her she was still in the house. "This case is going to give me a heart attack, I can already tell," I told Sandra.

"Daddy," Sandra asked. "Should we take a look at the attic, first?"

"We should," I admitted. "But I'm going to go ahead and build myself up to that." Brother, I know I've said this to you before, but sometimes this job takes a lot of courage that I do not readily have. Sandra, however, never seems afraid of anything. I don't know whether it's her condition or her own tenacity, but I'm really grateful for it regardless. She seemed absolutely ready to go to the root of the issue, and we both seemed to agree that whatever sent Kim to this house was in the attic. Ever since I saw that window, I just knew.

We spent some time setting up the equipment from the car. I didn't feel it was wise for this case to use the video cameras, but I had the EMF Meters and the recorders placed. Poltergeists tend to be the ones that are most talkative. I took Sandra out for dinner. I didn't feel comfortable in the house, or rather, I didn't feel comfortable having Sandra in the house. I felt like we were more in danger this time. Luckily, or unluckily, I have had a glimpse of her. She would likely be more active than others, which meant we may finish the case sooner. I have to admit, I was hesitant about the case from the beginning, but the family was willing to pay really, really well.

Sandra and I enjoyed a meal at a little sit-down restaurant and had some of the local food. I ordered in the native language, but I was so rusty at it that the waitress stifled a laugh and gave me a 'good try' sort of gesture. I turned my attention to Sandra. "So, Sandra, this poltergeist has a history of possessing people in their sleep. We need to make a code with each other. It has to be something to say 'I'm okay,' or 'I have it under control,' That way if the other doesn't respond, we'll know they're being influenced."

Sandra looked up at me. "Daddy, what if she learns our code and then says it for us?"

"There's no danger of that," I assured her. "Spirits don't have thought or will anymore. They're solely habitual." I didn't know if that was entirely the case, but I knew enough to know that a spirit can't learn a habit and copy it. It's like they're frozen in the time they've passed on; they can't take in new information. The best that can be done is to do something which lays the spirit to rest. Poltergeists have always been the hardest to do that with.

I leaned a bit closer. "Okay, so how about if one of us thinks the other is possessed, we'll say 'how's the weather?' And the other person would say, 'warm' if they're fine and 'cold' if not. If the other person says nothing at all, we'll take it as 'cold,' okay?"

Sandra nodded and shrugged. I watched her fiddle with the napkin and wondered if maybe there was something wrong. I grinned, "Here, let's test it now. I'll pretend to be possessed, and you ask the question. Ready?"

She looked at me, and I stiffened my body before wiggling my arms and making silly noises. She grinned. "How is the weather?"

I kept jiggling my arms and leaning my body around, "Wwwwaaaaah wh-waaaarrrrrmmmmmmmm." I reached over to her and started to tickle her sides and she started laughing. She tried to swat me away, and I knew I was making a scene in the restaurant but I didn't care. I was playing with my daughter, and she was having a great time.

We ate our dinner, and though there wasn't much food I was stuffed. I even got Sandra to eat everything on her plate even though it usually took begging and pleading to do so. We got back to the house, and the ominous darkness of the two-story house plus attic and basement sent a shiver up my spine. I took a moment to look at the windows to see if I could see anyone in them. I didn't, but Sandra seemed to. She gasped, "I saw her." Sandra pointed to the attic window. "She was there, wearing a white dress."

"She is in the attic, huh," I sighed. "Sandra, let's sleep in the same room tonight. I don't want us splitting up in this house."

"Okay," Sandra nodded. We walked up together and opened the door. I turned on the living room light and felt a little better. I wanted to turn on every light in the house, but doing that would make the poltergeist feel cornered and that might lead to being more violent. I looked over to the EMF meters by the front door and at the kitchen window, and they had some activity. I took the recording from the living room and, with Sandra sitting beside me on the couch, started to listen to it back. There was low static at first, nothing too sinister. As I kept listening, about the time that Sandra and I had left to eat, I heard words. I stopped it, played it back, and tried to hear what she was saying. It was in the native language. Luckily, or unluckily for me, they were simple words to decipher.

"I can see you, Derek."

I turned the recording off and wrote down the time in the tape that she spoke. I figured that was enough listening before bed. "Well, I'm thoroughly spooked," I sighed. Sandra was already nodding off. I picked her up, turned on the lights to the hallway and then the downstairs bedroom, and laid Sandra down to sleep. The window to the room was boarded up. It must have been the master bedroom. I didn't think I was going to be able to sleep.

Luckily, Sandra and I both learned the art of sleeping with the lights on.

I woke up only a few hours later. It was 3:30 in the morning and I was groggy, but I shot up immediately when I noticed Sandra was gone. "Sandra," I breathed. I looked around but didn't see her. I went to the hallway and still didn't see her, but I heard mumbling. The voice was coming from the bathroom. 'Do I look pretty now, Derek?'

My heart leaped and I swear it was like I had to swallow it back down. Sandra was in the darkness, staring at the bathroom mirror, muttering to herself.

"My hair is like strawberries and my eyes are gray. Don't you think I'm pretty now? I'm thinner and younger. Isn't this what you want?"

"Sandra," I cried out. I turned on the light as fast as I could, then Sandra jolted her body and spun around to look at me.

"Daddy?" She called.

I swallowed again. "Sweetie, how's the weather?"

She looked confused at first, but after blinking a few times she replied, "Warm."

I sighed and relaxed. "Honey, come on. Let's go back to bed." I held my hand out to her. Sandra looked over at the mirror for a second before hurrying to my hand and burying herself against my waist. I embraced her. "It's okay. It's going to be okay," I assured her.

We slept the rest of the night hugging each other. That way, I'd know for sure if she wiggled out in her sleep. Sandra was able to fall asleep, but I kept staring at the boarded-up window. I was exhausted come morning, but I wasn't about to let something happen to Sandra. I considered sleeping in a hotel nearby instead of sleeping in the actual house, and as you know Rory, I tend to feel like I have a better chance learning more about the beings when I spent nights with them. This woman had me spooked, Sandra had never been possessed before. It was the first time in weeks I thought about Lydia. I know you tell me to forget about it, Rory, but jobs like this always bring those memories back.

It was that moment when the poltergeist targeted Sandra when this haunting became personal. I thought about what Kim had said while she was in Sandra's body. What sort of sick, abusive psychological torture did Derek put her through to be so vengeful that she would take over the bodies of young woman apparently trying to appeal to a man who is long gone? Derek must have been a sick man, and it's ruined everything Kim might have been. The only question was, what did I have to do to free her of it? How could I get Kim to move on?

I delayed it for an entire day, but it was time to make it to the attic. I really didn't want to, and I wished that I knew someone nearby who could look after Sandra for me, but I was left to bring her up with me. Passing the other bedrooms on the second floor and, with recorder and a heat sensor in hand, we both wandered up to the dreaded top floor.

There wasn't much to see at first, the normal memories caked in dust and cobwebs. There was a lot of room to move around, the entire attic could almost be used as another functioning room of the house if it weren't for the fact that someone my height could only stand upright for a portion of it. Sandra could get around pretty easily. "Stay close," I muttered to her.

I heard static in the recorder and a chill up my spine. I halted, waited for the feeling to pass, then played back the recording.

"Good to see you, Derek," The whisper came dripping through the recorder in the native language. Sandra jumped. She turned her eyes wide at me.

"I'm not Derek, Kim. My name is Princeton," I replied. My breath caught in my throat from how cold it got around me, and there was a louder static. "Liar," The recorder shouted when I played back. "Do you want to see how pretty I can be for you?"

I hesitated, "Not really."

Sandra's head threw back and she gasped. I dropped the instruments which started to go haywire to hold onto her shoulders. "Sandra. Sandra sweetie, how's the weather?"

Sandra kept gasping, her body jolting. I was worried that she would give herself whiplash. "W-warm," She managed to say.

"Let's go back downstairs, okay? Sandra?" I pleaded.

She wrenched her body away from me. "Sandra," I cried. Sandra hurried to a quilt and pulled at it. Dust and mold floated everywhere, and I had to close my eyes from the sudden glare. The light of the mid-day sun bounced off of a reflective surface, now free from the quilt.

"Why don't you notice me?" I heard Sandra's plea. "You care about me so little, brushing me off like I was an annoyance."

My heart leaped out again. I know it was Kim talking to Derek, but I swear I heard Lidia in Sandra's voice. "I'm sorry," I told her. I didn't know what else to say.

The dust settled. I coughed for a few seconds, trying to see Sandra through fogged up glasses. I had to take them off. "Sandra."

"Warm," She replied.

I had to get Kim out of Sandra somehow. It was breaking me to watch her jerk and twitch, trying to keep some control. Once my vision could make out clearer shapes, I realized that I was standing before a full body mirror. Sandra stood before it but the reflection wasn't her. It was the face of a mangled bride, black hair matted in blood and jaw slack. I could see Sandra's face in profile as she tried to turn towards me. She was crying. I could see her mouth trying to make out a word.

"C-co-c-old."

"Let go of her, dammit!" I shouted. "Let my daughter go!"

I had a flashback just then. I remembered having to say those words before. My body turned cold, I felt dizzy, I couldn't think straight. "She's my daughter too," I heard a voice say. The voice was familiar, and it was a voice I've tried so hard to forget. I couldn't tell who was standing in front of me. I saw a short, plump woman with short black hair and a wedding gown, then I saw a little girl with strawberry hair and gray eyes, and then I saw a blonde-haired woman with blue eyes and red lips. I knew all these faces, but I kept going back and forth from recognizing them to not being able to recognize them at all. I heard echoes all around me.

"Go ahead and shoot!" I heard someone say. Was it me? I can't remember. Then I heard a bang. Just like that, my eyes shot open.

"Daddy," Sandra cried. She was looking down at me, shaking. I was so overwhelmed, I sat up and embraced her. I felt a blanket fall from over my shoulders and the feel of cold hardwood beneath me. We were still in the attic. It was getting dark. The mirror was covered up again.

I pulled Sandra away and looked her over. She didn't seem to have any cuts or bruises. "Sandra, sweetheart, are you okay? What happened?"

Sandra sniffed and tried to speak cohesively through her tears. "You were shouting at the mirror, and you were jerking around, then when I put the quilt over the mirror again you fell over and wouldn't wake up. I thought you died daddy, I was so scared."

I pulled her close to me and hugged her. "I'm okay," I assured her. "Everything is fine, we're going to be fine."

We spent the night at a nearby hotel. We needed a good night's rest and I needed to think. While Sandra was asleep, my head was invaded by thoughts. I didn't know how much I said about Lidia while I was being possessed. I was terrified she'd start asking questions. I decided that I was going to fly her to you for the rest of the summer. What happened that night, I couldn't let it happen again. My heart can only break so many times. Sandra is the most important thing to me in this whole world, and I know its selfish of me to take her with me to these dangerous cases on her breaks. For her sake, I had to end it.

Breakfast was served at the hotel lobby. Sandra and I ate in silence for a little while. Eventually, I broke the silence. "Sandra, I had a bit of thinking. Your uncle Rory might need some help writing the archives for our demon and spirit sightings. We can fly you out tonight to go see him."

She didn't answer, just pushed her food around with her fork.

"I'm sure he'll be really happy to see you," I said.

"Daddy, mom is dead, right?"

My whole body tingled. "Yes, sweetheart."

"Was she shot?"

"No, she wasn't shot," I told her. "Remember, I told you how she was sick. Why are we talking about this?"

Sandra shrugged, unable to make any eye contact. I ate a bit of food. "I'm flying you out to your uncle Rory."

"Today is your last day on the case, isn't it?" She asked.

"I can ask to extend the case a bit longer," I explained. "It's more important you're taken somewhere safe."

There was more silence.

"Well, somebody shot somebody," Sandra muttered.

My body tensed.

"I think Derek shot Kimmy. He called her ugly a lot. And fat, and old, and stupid. He told her she 'looked better this way' after she died. Derek was an awful person."

My body relaxed. I looked down at my plate. "Yeah. Unfortunately... There are a lot of awful people in this world."

"She thinks you're Derek." Sandra looked up at me, "You're

not awful at all, daddy."

My eyes trailed to her before she looked away again. I smiled. "I'm glad you think so."

She fell silent again. I could tell she was trying to find the right words for what she wanted to say, so I ate and remained patient.

"Derek never paid attention to her," She muttered. My eyes trailed off to the side.

"I think she just needs to be told she's pretty."

"Honey, I really don't think it's going to be that simple," I assured her.

Sandra shrugged again. "It seems pretty simple to me."

"Does it now?" I asked.

"Daddy, I don't want to go back to uncle Rory's. I want to stay here with you and help with stuff."

"Sweetheart, I can't have you around that house and that mirror. I'll get too worried about you, and if something were to happen," I started.

"Please, daddy. I like doing this with you, and it's the only time I get to see you."

My heart wrenched for a moment. I looked down, I couldn't look at her.

"Just try to compliment her today, and if that doesn't work then I'll go see uncle Rory. Just try it, please?"

I took a moment to consider it. It was unlikely that all that needed to be done was compliment Kim, but it wasn't impossible. Still, I couldn't bear the thought of Sandra going back into the house. I couldn't leave an 11-year-old in a hotel by herself in a strange place for a day, either.

"Fine, it's a deal. But you have to stay in the car, doors all locked and you are not to leave the car under any circumstances, okay?"

Sandra looked down at her plate and nodded, a light smile on her face.

We arrived at the house once more. I locked all the doors and started for the door. Before entering the house, I turned around and made a heart symbol with my hands to my daughter. Sandra made a heart symbol back to me. I took a deep breath, clenched my fists and rushed back into the house.

Strange as it may seem, I always felt brave when I had Sandra around with me. The cases during the breaks are always the hardest because I don't have someone like Sandra to keep me focused on why I keep doing these jobs. Now that I stood in the building all alone, despite it being mid-day, I felt ready to run out screaming at any moment. Regardless, I kept moving on upstairs.

Every step I took, I listened for any extra noises. It was silent besides the settling house and my own ragged breathing. I worried that Kim may be waiting until dark. I was also worried that, perhaps she didn't leave mine or Sandra's body at all and she remained dormant in one of us. Just the idea of this poltergeist still possessing Sandra made my teeth clench. I didn't have these thoughts for long, however, since by the time I got to the attic I felt the familiar chill. I shakily wandered into the middle of the room to retrieve the tape recorder that has since run out of film. I took the tape out, pocketed it, and put in a new tape to use. I pressed 'record,' and I started to talk to her.

"Kim, are you here?"

The recorder picked up static, and I played it back.

"Go away."

I clenched my fist, trying to steady my voice. "Kim, I need to talk to you. Listen, I understand you've been hurt."

"You hurt me, Derek."

I took in a sharp breath. "Yes. I'm sorry I hurt you, Kim. I didn't deserve you. Please, forget about me and move on."

I felt a chill run through me.

"Murderer. You hurt me. You killed me. Was I so ugly that you couldn't bear to see my face?"

The blanket fell off of the covered mirror.

"Look at my face! Look at what you've created!"

I turned to the mirror to see a disheveled bride before me, short and stout with black matted hair and a screaming face. It twitched and spasmed as she looked at me. My breath caught in my throat and for a moment, it was hard to breathe.

"I'm sorry," Was all I could say. Now as I took a closer look at her, I saw the stain of tears. Dried blood flaked on one side of her head. I took a step closer to the mirror. Before my eyes, her image had changed. My chest stung at the transformation, her stout posture became tall and voluptuous. Her black matted hair flowed to blond. It's been eight years since I'd last seen Lydia, but her vision was as clear as ever.

"You neglected me."

"Yes, I," I admitted. "I never meant to hurt you."

"Excuses!" She shouted.

"But it's true," I assured her. "We were young and I was reckless and stupid and too caught up in my work. I took you for granted, called you horrible things, and in the end I knew I was to blame. But don't let me keep you away from happiness. Please," I shook my head. I had to remember why I was here. "You have to move on."

"You took everything from me," Lydia, or Kim, cried.

"I did. Nothing can change what's been done. As much as I wish, how I wish we could reset the world if even to fix just one mistake. But here we are, this is how it is." I blinked hard and kept myself on track as best as I could, but Lydia still stood before me. "I lied to you. The truth is, Kim, you're beautiful."

"How dare you say that to me now," She whispered.

"I know I'm late in saying it," I closed my eyes desperately. When I opened them again, Kim stood before me once more. "You always were very beautiful. You're also very smart." She was smart enough as a spirit anyway, to use my own insecurities against me. I never met a spirit to do that before.

That was when I noticed the image before me changing again. This time, there were small differences. The jolting happened less often. The blood was fading away. "And," I continued. "You're absolutely radiant in that gown." The dress mended itself as I said that. I straightened up.

"Your hair seems so soft to the touch," Kim's hair fell from its former matted state. "Your face is soft, too." Well I never said I was good at complimenting women, but it seemed to work all the same. "Your eyes," The sockets faded and were replaced with black eyes and long lashes. "They remind me of a deer. They're graceful and filled with wonder."

She smiled.

I felt my shoulders relax, and I smiled back. "Derek was an idiot to have taken your beauty for granted. You never meant to cause pain to anyone, but you were hurting so much yourself that you couldn't bear to endure it alone. All you needed was for someone to see the true beauty you had all along." I've always wondered if that was why poltergeists existed. They've been wronged so badly that they couldn't possibly move on with all the hatred left here in the physical world. We know that a soul gets connected to what they were close to when they were alive. "You must have looked at this mirror a million times for your soul to get stuck here, wanting so badly to be able to convince yourself that you weren't worthless. You just wanted Derek to see you for who you were."

The ghost kept smiling, silent tears rolling down her face. She fell to her knees and covered her face with her hands.

Hesitantly, I sank to my knees as well. "You don't need someone like that bounding you down here. Kimmy, I mean this sincerely. You are a very beautiful woman. It was Derek who tore you down and made you ugly. But you don't need to keep existing this way. You have the right to be yourself, this kind soul that only wanted a little recognition from someone she loved. I'll say what he should have for you. You look positively stunning in that gown."

I couldn't hear her voice over the recorder anymore. I watched as she lifted her head and looked directly at me, her sweet smile beaming through hundred-year-old tears. Her mouth formed the words, I was confused at first, but then I realized it was 'Thank you' in her natural language. I nodded to her in response. There was a beam of light, she looked up to the sky, and then she was gone.

Rory, I'd like to go back to my question now. Am I risking Sandra's life taking her on these cases with me? Am I being selfish wanting to spend time with her while I'm working on her holidays from school? Not a day goes by that I don't worry being a bad father, but I'm worried about what Sandra might have heard while I was being possessed. She knows that talking about her mother makes me upset, and I'm worried she'll find out eventually. But I also don't want to neglect her like I did Lydia. I don't want to shut Sandra out of my life. I want her to be with me to share the thrill of this world that I encounter regularly. She wants to be here, and I don't want to force her away, but am I being irresponsible? Probably. I await your reply, and I hope this letter finds you well. Sandra says hello.

With love, Princeton

THE LICKER

The Licker is an odd little yokai. It's one of those ancient, common spirits that have a lot of legends, but not many people want to talk about them. I didn't even know what it was until I encountered it myself. One night, as I was rushing to the bathroom in my house, I see something in the darkness. It was hunched over the toilet, moving, breathing. I turned on the light and it just disappeared. I was terrified, but I couldn't NOT go to the bathroom. I left the door open in case of a quick getaway, but nothing happened. I wondered if I imagined it.

The next day, I told my friend Kenji about it. His eyes lit up like fireworks. "Yokai," Was the first thing he said.

"In my bathroom?" I crossed my arms.

"Listen, Satu-chan- "

"don't call me that."

"There are sandal yokai. SANDALS. I would not be surprised if your gross bathroom had a neglected item that turned into a demon."

"Kenji, you don't know my bathroom. You've never even been to my house yet and I've lived there for almost six months now."

"I've been busy teaching. I'm a teacher," He decided to remind me. "If I were a comic-book artist like you I'd have all the time in the world to visit but I have to actually grade papers and do work."

I glared at him. He liked to pretend I lived a charmed life scrambling from deadline to deadline making peanuts for my talent only to get ridiculed like it isn't an actual job. He knew it irked me. I tried to not let it show, but his grin was too stupid.

"I hate you," I told him.

"You love me," He beamed. "But Satoru, honestly, I think you have a yokai in your bathroom."

"Oh yeah," I challenged. "What kind of yokai?"

Kenji shrugged. "I dunno, I didn't see it. Why don't you look it up?"

"I will if I see it again," I dismissed. I honestly thought that I may have imagined it so I didn't press the matter much. We spent the rest of our lunch at the school he worked at talking about his students and some of the staff and a guy he really liked. I told him to go for it, but like usual he brushed it off and preferred to retract into his fantasies. He insisted I meet someone but I was never really someone who took relationships that seriously. I didn't see the appeal. Kenji was really my only social life and I was content with spending the rest of my time alone in my house with my dog and my cat. "I live vicariously through you," I told him. "So, you're the one that's gotta get himself in a relationship soon."

"I'm still a little hurt from when I dated Rika," He admitted. "She was just awful. What if this guy is actually an awful person?"

"You won't know until you try," I urged.

"Naw, I'll just pretend I asked and he rejected me already, cut out the embarrassing middle part." He sipped his soda.

"You're hopeless," I informed him with a smirk.

"Not as hopeless as you, Satu-chan," He joked.

I picked up my chopsticks. "If you don't stop calling me that I'm eating your dumpling."

He guarded his dumpling and huffed. "Don't take other's food, that's rude."

"I can't believe you're a teacher with how immature you are," I laughed.

The next morning went on as usual, and the morning after. A deadline was coming up to have the final inking for a new comic and I hadn't slept well the night before, so when I saw the shadow in my bathroom again, I was sure that it was an illusion. Like before, it was gone as fast as it came.

I didn't dare tell Kenji about the second sighting. He was a huge fan of mythology and I didn't feel like listening to him talk about yokai again. He was so invested in the idea of demons that he went to the Ningyo Kuyo festival every year, which was the festival of respectfully burning toys so they won't get possessed from abandonment. Kenji liked coming back and giving me silly little souvenirs from it, which I keep in a little drawer of things that will never be useful in my life. Every so often I'd take something out for my cat Orenji or my dog Ringo to play with.

It wasn't like I disbelieved in yokai, I just had little interest in the topic. I was too caught up in my work to feel like the hallucination I have when going to my bathroom at night was anything pertinent. Then one night, as I was cuddled in my blanket, I heard Ringo losing his mind. He kept yapping and growling, and when the idea of an intruder came to mind, I shot awake as soon as I could. I could see its silhouette from the nightlight by my door.

Ringo was barking at it from the doorway, but it hunched there, clinging to the ceiling nearly over my bed, licking my wall with a large tongue. "Ugh," I shouted and hurried to my desk-lamp. I turned it on, and it was gone. Ringo stopped barking.

I looked at my dog. "You saw it, too?" I realized then that it couldn't be only a hallucination. I closed the bedroom door so Ringo would stay in my room to bark in case it came back, but I could barely sleep after that. Eventually, Ringo jumped onto my bed and slept against my hip. I tried not to think about the husky fur I'll have to brush off of my bed later, but any other thought was welcome to whatever had been on my ceiling.

Caving in, I searched the internet for yokai with large tongues. An akaname, I found out, is a creature that licks filthy bathrooms at night. At first, I was relieved, but then I was insulted. "My bathroom isn't that filthy. If that was the demon I saw, then why was it licking my wall?" My body shuddered.

"You know, I would say 'I told you so,' but I feel almost like it's self-explanatory at this point," Kenji joked.

"I shouldn't have told you," I muttered. "Well, how do I get rid of it?"

"It's obvious, isn't it?" Kenji pointed his chopsticks at me. "You have to clean your bathroom."

"It's not even that filthy," I cried.

"Tell that to the yokai," Kenji countered.

I huffed. "Why me, though? I'm sure there are plenty other filthy bathrooms that are worse than mine."

"Well I can't say, I've never seen your bathroom."

The rest of the afternoon was spent cleaning my bathroom. By the time I finished cleaning, it was spotless. "There. See the yokai find any dirt or grime in this bathroom," I smiled.

That night, I didn't sleep for very long. I wanted to see if my house was finally yokai-less. My cat slept at my windowsill, her tail twitching as she took peace in the moonlight. I envied her.

It was the middle of the night and I decided at last to go take a look at the bathroom. I was as quiet as I could be, walking slowly, hopeful that there was nothing there to be worried about. To my horror, and to my frustration, it remained there hunched over, licking the same spot behind my toilet. "Hey," I shouted and turned on the light. The yokai disappeared. I walked up to the spot it was licking but I saw only the clean wall tile I had scrubbed just yesterday. I groaned out of frustration. On my way to my room, I could see the yokai licking at the ceiling of my bedroom again. I turned on the light and it disappeared. "This is ridiculous," I shouted.

I slept with the lights on. It was uncomfortable and I woke up with a headache, but it was a better alternative to having a creature hovering over my bed in my sleep. I was out of ideas.

"That is weird. It says in the book that they only eat filth, right? So why would the akaname still be in your house if you cleaned everything? Could it be a different yokai?"

"I looked," I told Kenji. "But nothing else seemed to fit what it is. I'm starting to get a little scared."

Kenji looked to me. "Listen, Satu-chan. If it's that bad for you then I'll see what I can do about coming over this weekend and spending the night so I can catch a glimpse of this thing. Maybe with the two of us thinking about a solution, we'll be able to get rid of the yokai."

Despite him using the horrid nickname, I could tell Kenji was sincere about my feelings. I sighed and lightly punched his arm. "Stop using that nickname already, it's embarrassing."

"I think it's cute," Kenji replied. "And it suits you."

"It does not," I blushed. "You're always picking on me."

"That's what brothers do, right?" He winked. He always fancied as being like a brother to me, and I guess I really never had an argument against it.

My grin widened and I said in the cutest, most annoying way possible, "Onii-san."

Kenji physically shuddered. "Ugh, I've created a monster." We both laughed.

Kenji arrived at my house on Saturday. I cleaned the entire house until it was spotless. He came by and whistled, "You're really serious about this cleaning thing. I can't see a speck of dust anywhere." I puffed my chest out in pride.

We spent the day watching television and talking and doing all the things we used to do together as kids. Ringo and Orenji joined us on the couch. Orenji purred and kneaded Kenji's leg before sleeping on his lap. "I was thinking," Kenji said. "What if the filth isn't in your house, but in your walls? Could it be that maybe you have mold in the wall?"

My heart dropped. "It would cost a lot of money to fix that if it spread all over the bathroom and the bedroom." The more I thought about it, the more I was sure that was what it was. I thought I should probably see about getting someone here to fix that, but I only just got on top of my bills.

"You know, if we were room-mates in a house then living expenses would be cheaper for both of us," Kenji pointed out.

"We tried to be room-mates before, remember? You were going to try to kill me with all my snoring," I reminded him.

"Well, we didn't know each other well enough yet," He pointed out. "I think we'll do better next time."

"Maybe," I contemplated.

That night, Kenji and I waited in my room with the lights turned off. I kept looking at the ceiling, he kept looking towards the hallway. Ringo and Orenji scurried around the house. I sighed, "I'm going to throw a toy out for them to play with. They'll be quiet hopefully."

"Sure, I'll wait here," Kenji replied.

I walked out the door and towards the kitchen. I grabbed a little souvenir from the festival and tossed it over to them. On my way back, I froze. The akaname was glued to the side of the wall, licking the living room. I hurried to the bedroom. "Kenji, it's in the living room," I hissed.

"What, really?" He asked. He followed me there and he almost cried out in surprise. "Yah- My God it's huge," He hissed back. "It's like the size of a horse."

"It wasn't that big before," I whispered. I grabbed Kenji's arm and scrambled for the switch.

Kenji stopped my hand. "Wait. Maybe if we hit the wall there with a hammer or something, we can see what's causing the akaname to try licking there."

"Are you insane, you want to hit holes in my wall?" I hissed incredulously.

"The mold guys will be doing that anyway. I'll help you patch it up if it turns out to be nothing, okay?"

I didn't like the idea at all, but I also didn't see there being much more of a choice. It was either that or move, and I wasn't prepared to do that when I got this house for so cheap. I should have known something was wrong when the landlord wanted so little to sell it. I was still making payments, but the house would be paid off in the span of a year. I went to the kitchen and took a hammer out of the junk drawer. When I came back, Kenji's eyes were on Orenji. "Is that the yokai keychain I got you last year at the festival?"

I ignored him. "When I turn on the light, you hit the wall with the hammer. Try not to destroy the wall too much, please?"

"I'll make the hole as clean and small as possible," He promised. I snuck closer to the living room light, and once I turned the light on Kenji came by and hit the hammer right where the akaname just was. There was a loud 'bang,' and to my surprise the wall just gave in. Kenji peeled away parts of the broken wall. "What the," He peered in more.

His eyes went wide. He scrambled back, falling over and dropping the hammer. He cried out, and a large chunk of the wall peeled down. Between the wall was a mass of bones, matted hair and flesh. The stomach had been hollowed out, the skin looked wrinkled and dried, as though it had been prepared or something. Kenji and I both lost a battle with our stomachs. I cried out in horror.

"Let's get out of here," Kenji cried. But I was struck with realization. I grabbed the hammer from Kenji and ran to my room. The cat and the dog both ran out of the room when they saw me come in. I stood on my bed and hit the ceiling. "What are you doing, let's just go!" Kenji tried to stop me, but one more hit before he dragged me away let the skeletal remains loose to fall onto my bed. I cried and screamed. I was in hysterics. Kenji had to drag me out of the room, the sight of the yokai licking my bathroom wall being the last sight I registered before blacking out.

Kenji called the police. He took me to his house and even braved the house of murder long enough to get Ringo and Orenji as well as some of my clothes. There were weeks of interrogations. A hunt for my landlord began.

People ask me all the time when they find out I was the woman that lived in that house why I didn't smell the formaldehyde. They ask me how I couldn't have known, why I wasn't suspicious of my landlord. You don't think to be aware of things like that. I've never smelled formaldehyde before, I had no reason to be suspicious. In the rush of everyday life, who would stop to wonder if there were skeletons in their walls? If it weren't for the yokai, I might have never known.

STRANGE NEW PLACE

I heard the whistle. It echoed out my window, and I felt my heart race. It beckoned me to it. It whistled again. I didn't know why, but it sounded persistent. It echoed in my head more and more, I didn't even know if it was still whistling by the time I grabbed my coat and went out the door.

The train station wasn't far behind, just a small creek and a short distance into the woods away. There weren't many passenger trains anymore. The most I expected as I crossed the creek was that I would see the cargo train chugging by and that would be the end of it. At the very least, it would settle my craving to see it. I don't think I ever lived anywhere where there wasn't a train track nearby. It was always something that I heard in the background, and most of the time I didn't think about it. Even as a child, when I would play in the playground as the afternoon traffic went by, the distant echo of the train whistle wasn't something I would normally pay attention to.

I didn't know why I was rustling my way through the tall grass and trees, or why the whistling of the train called out to me so much that I would leave the safety of my quiet home, but I was enjoying the crisp forest walk regardless. I supposed that I was at least getting in some exercise. I spent hours just sitting down in my living room after work, so at least it was getting me out of the house. My life was the carnival casino I worked at. I didn't spend time with my coworkers outside of the job, I didn't visit my family or even go out to eat most days. Before that moment, I hardly even explored anything past my yard. I was eager and afraid at the same time, but my legs wouldn't stop walking.

Once I got there, I didn't recognize the vehicle waiting at the station. It was long, white and sleek like an electrical bullet train but I didn't see how it could operate on coal-run tracks. Was this some sort of new model? If so, why was it stopping in a rural area near a small town in the middle of the night? It was a passenger train, even.

There was no one around, which was odd. I expected there to be workers or passengers or anyone, but I was strangely all alone. The door slid open, and there was a brilliant light. I shied away from it, but it left me with a soft, warm glow. I felt drawn to it, like prey to an angler's glow. I drug myself right into the jaws of the predator, unaware that I was never going home again.

I don't know how much time passed before I was able to shake away the light from my mind. My vision returned to me. "Welcome, welcome, step right up. Jazzer's the name, and this is my domain."

The being that greeted me was like one that I've seen in my nightmares. He had no face, just a wide, toothy grin. He flipped his cane and gave a carnival bow. "You came just in time for your trip, George."

"How did you know my name," I asked with a heavy breath. The train jolted into motion and I had to grab a rail.

"This train has two destinations," Jazzer leaned against his cane. "There is your destination, and then NOT your destination." He pointed to the front and the back of the train. "Choose wisely."

Then he disappeared. I was left there wondering what to do, when I realized that out the windows, it didn't look as though we were moving at all. Despite that, I felt the ground rumbling beneath me and the inertia of the train was pushing me back.

Back. Wait. Go back. I decided to run to the back of the train and try to get out before the train went too far away from home. I ran as fast as I could from one cart to another cart. I shouted, "Help, someone stop the train! I want to go back home!" But there was no one to hear me. I ran to the next cart and fell over from the rumbling train. I felt like I could almost slide from cart to cart. I looked out the window, but everything still looked exactly the same. I felt hopeless, the train was just jerking me wherever it wanted. I had no control. I remained on the ground, hopeless. What would happen if I just stayed here? Would the train send me back home out of boredom? Or would I just be stuck here forever? "Jazzer!" I cried to the front of the train. "Please, just let me go home!"

The train halted suddenly, and I felt myself fly backwards. I hit my head on the door of the cab. Well, at least I knew for a fact now that this wasn't a dream. I sat up slowly to see Jazzer standing before me. "Look, you have a very nice train," I told him. "But I really want to go home, now."

"You want to change your destination? You'll have to play a game, first." Behind him popped up a fair game booth blocking the way to the next cart. It had three darts sitting on the counter and a wheel of colors on the other side. It looked just like one of the casino games I maintained at work.

"Step right up and choose where to go. You get three chances!"

The lack of expressions on the creature's face other than his eerie grin made me shiver. I stood up, rubbing my head, and hesitantly got closer to him to see the 'game.' The wheel had a lot of different colors in different hues. Each section was so small that I wasn't sure what was good and what was bad. I leaned forward a little, I could barely make out words on each section. Even the words that were short enough to decipher were of things I never heard before. How was I supposed to know what to aim for?"

"Take your three shots, George," Jazzer jeered. "The audience is waiting."

Audience? I looked around but I didn't see anyone. Now that he said that, I kept having the feeling of being watched. I took a deep breath and nodded, "Okay…"

I picked up the first dart and was about to throw it when the wheel started to spin. "Oh come on," I sighed. Well, it wasn't like I knew what I was choosing anyway. I held my breath and threw one dart. I heard it go 'Thunk,' but the wheel was spinning so much that I couldn't see where it was pointing. I threw the other dart, 'Thunk,'but I wouldn't tell where it was until the wheel stopped spinning. I tossed the last dart as straight as I could. The wheel slowed down, but as it did the wheel was only two colors. Red and blue. Two slots. All three darts were on the red half, 'Not your destination.'

"Oh, come ON," I cried.

"Sorry kid, them's the rules," Jazzer cackled before he and the game disappeared. The train jerked and started to speed again. I hurried towards the back of the cart again.

"No, I can't just never go home again. My parents will find out, they'll find you! They'll call the police!" I shouted. "This is a kidnapping!" I managed to get myself to another cart where there was what seemed like a route map. I gripped a hand rail and looked to it, but as I did, I noticed that all except for one route read 'Not your Destination.' I focused on the one that said 'Your Destination.' "How do I get there? There has to be a way, there's got to be a way to better my odds." I saw something jump around on the map. I thought it was a fly, at first, but then I noticed that it was a 'You are Here' sticker. Carelessly bouncing here and there almost too quick to keep an eye on. It didn't follow any path, no paths, just bouncing and turning and spinning around. I tried to hit it, to move it on my own, but a thick wall of plastic shielded the sticker from me. I had no control. I turned back to the rest of the cart and shouted, "You can't keep me here forever!"

There was no response. I was losing whatever composure I had left. I kept going back from cart to cart, trying to find something different, or an ending, or anything. "What do you want, huh? Money? I'll get you all the money you want! I'll rob a bank if you need me to, just let me go home! Is it company? Or hey, if you want to play another game, I'm down for that, too! Come on, just tell me what you want!"

The train stopped and I fell backward. I was at the last cart, though I thought I was in the middle before. The door slid open. I thought my heart was going to rip out of my chest. My lungs felt like they were burning, I scrambled out of the train and ran off of the platform. The door closed, and the train started to leave again. I watched it go and sighed.

I got out. At last. It felt like it happened so fast, I explored the hope that it may have all just been a dream. I laid down on the grass and took in the fresh air. I opened my eyes to look at the black sky.

Odd, the night was more black than usual. Maybe my eyes needed to adjust to the light. It was darker than usual, too. Were there clouds out tonight?

I sat up. No, something wasn't right. I wandered a little way to a clearing to get a better look.

A lone white moon shone above me. My eyes widened. "No, that isn't right," I cried. "The moon is too small. And where's the other moon?!" I looked through the sky, "All the stars are different, I don't see any blue or red ones, they're all just white! They're not in the right places, where's the Smiling Man constellation?!" I had to be seeing things, I rushed home as fast as I could. Trees and bushes were all arranged differently. I heard a strange sound of chirping that I couldn't recognize. I got to the creek, and it was flowing the opposite way. I ran home as fast as I could. "Someone help me!" I screamed. I hoped that my house was at least the same, that my phone would still be on the counter, that my parent's numbers were still the same. I tried to open my door with my key and it worked to my relief. Once I got inside, however,

I was face to face with a woman I'd never met before. "George honey, where have you been? You look pale."

"Pale?" I asked, and I looked down to my hands. "Ah!" I yelped. "My skin!" My skin was pale and almost pink. It wasn't gray at all. "Oh, my Almighty, am I sick?!"

"Almighty who?" The woman asked. "George, you're scaring me."

"Who are you," I asked. "Where am I? What year is this?"

The woman tried to get close to me, but I shied away. "I'm your wife, George. Don't you remember me? Listen, just sit down okay? I'll call the ambulance."

"A wife? That's impossible," I demanded.

"George, you're scaring me," The woman's voice shook.

"You're scared?! I'm 23 years old and you're saying we're married?!"

"Twenty-three years old? George," The woman implored. "Please, relax. We'll figure this out, okay? You must have hit your head and suffered some amnesia. You're forgetting nearly seventeen years of your life."

"No, I'm not, I was in this train and this guy, well, THING, he took me and," I could feel my eyes getting hot with tears.

"Sweetheart, please. Just sit down and listen to me. You're not 23 anymore. You're going on 40 now. It's 2010, sweetheart."

"2010?!" I hollered. "It was 1993 just hours ago!"

"Just relax, I'll call the hospital and we'll get this all sorted out, okay? I can make you some tea to calm you down."

Exhausted, confused, and frustrated, I sat down and wrapped myself in a blanket. "Alright," I said, but honestly, I was just worried I was going to pass out if I kept trying to find out what happened.

When the police came, I tried as calm as possible to explain what happened. Of course, nobody believed me. I was sent to a hospital. They decided that I may have suffered a concussion. My head was still bruised from hitting it in the train. I told the story of Jazzer to anyone that would listen, but even though I had people interested in the story no one believed it. I was getting tired reliving the same events over and over again.

I've been placed into therapy twice a week. The continents, the islands, and all the monuments have changed. Names have changed. No one has ever heard of Torusa or about the white train, and no one knows the name Jazzer. They think I made up a second moon. They think I am delirious in thinking that I was never married and that it's supposed to be 1993. My parents aren't the same, my coworkers aren't the same, but I still work at the Carnival Casino. I still work on the machines. It's the only place that I feel any familiarity. I keep worrying about my life back home. No matter how much I try to get used to things, I don't know this place. This world is not mine. What happened to me?

DOLLS DON'T FEEL

"Where am I?" He asked. "Why is everything so dark?"

He tried to move his body, but found that he couldn't. He felt groggy, like he was in a dream. He wondered if his eyes were closed, but he felt as though they were wide open. He couldn't blink. How did he get here?

"I can't remember my name," He muttered. "It was," His thoughts fell silent.

A little girl picked up the burlap sack doll that lay face-down on the couch and took it with her to her room. She looked fondly at him. He stared back with two different sized black buttons for eyes. He had a stitched-up mouth and messy black hair that covered his head and over his eyes. The little girl parted his hair to one side.

He could see a little girl that was much bigger than he was with pink eyes and hair. Her skin was pale, almost ghostly white. She beamed at him and held him close. He found that he couldn't move at all. "What's going on?" He tried to ask, but not only could he make no sound but he could not muster up any clear thought or emotion. It was as though he knew it was a dream and he would wake up soon. He was not aware that he would never wake up.

"You're my new best friend, Runner," She told the doll.

"Is Runner my name," The doll wondered.

"Ophelia, time for dinner!" A voice called from downstairs.

"Uh-oh," Ophelia replied. She took great care in setting Runner on her bed, propping him up on a pillow. "I have to go eat now, but I'll be right back." She kissed his eye, but he didn't feel anything. "Bye bye, Runner!" She hurried away, little black dress-shoes tapping on the hardwood floor.

"Something is wrong," Runner realized. He kept trying to move, but he was too tired, or perhaps too dizzy. He couldn't gather any energy to speak or move or even motivate himself to panic about it. He was strangely calm. He couldn't remember being anything else or anyone else, but he could feel enough to know that something was different. Who was Ophelia?

Runner could look only straight ahead. He noticed the room was full of black fabric and white lace. Religious symbols hung on the wall, her closet full of dresses and cute polished shoes. There were other dolls and stuffed animals around. Too many. Runner decided that there needed to be less toys around.

Ophelia came back upstairs and picked Runner up, holding him in her arms and showing him parts of her room as though she were a tour guide. She introduced him to every other stuffed animal. She took him to a plush dog and pig. "This is Rudolph, and this is Ginger. I had Ginger since I was a very little girl so be nice, okay? These are all my pictures that I drew." The drawings were hard to tell what they were besides scribbles of orange and red. "This is a picture of when I scraped my knee at the playground. It was really scary because there was blood everywhere." The girl pointed to a drawing of pink and red. The red covered almost the entire page. She took Runner to the foot of her bed where a white box lay. "This is a health kit. Papi calls it that and says to use it if I ever start bleeding again until he or mami gets there. I lose a lot of blood because I'm very sick," She said. "But I have you now!" She cried. "And you'll protect me, right?"

She smiled at Runner. Runner wanted to smile back, but the stitches wouldn't move. Was this his purpose?

Ophelia took a lot of naps throughout the day. She held Runner close to her as she slept. Runner laid there, immobile, looking at the other toys that Ophelia had. It filled him with an emotion more powerful than he remembered having. He wanted to tear apart every other toy until he was all there was. Runner kept his focus on the dog that Ophelia named Rudolph. The stuffed dog had a little brown nose and floppy ears, and sat up on its rear legs as though it were a bear cub. Its large glass eyes stared dully back at him. Runner wanted to tear the eyes out. He desired to reach at Rudolph and tear him to shreds. His rage and desperation manifested two large, long clawed shadows that slithered their way across the carpet without a sound towards the rival plush object. The claws scratched at Rudolph, leaving gashes on the fabric. The stuffing fell out and Runner was satisfied, but very tired. The large shadows retracted, and Runner fell dormant again.

Ophelia woke up and kissed Runner's head. She opened her eyes to see Rudolph's stuffing scattered everywhere. She cried out and sat up in bed. "No, Rudolph!" She cried. Pouting, eyes full of tears, she turned Runner to face her. "Did you hurt Rudolph? Why? That's not a very nice thing to do! You get a time-out!" She set Runner down on the bed and hurried to her mom with the shredded dog to see if she could fix him. When her mother lamented that Rudolph was too far damaged, Ophelia held a little funeral for Rudolph with all the toys attending except for Runner. She cried and hoped that Rudolph would be happy in the plush and plastic afterlife.

Runner woke up by the time Ophelia finished with the funeral. He saw Ophelia's eyes glossy with tears. A new powerful emotion came over him.

When night came upon them, Ophelia told Runner, "I forgive you because you didn't know. But don't hurt any more of my toys. The man in the alley said you needed a place to belong but you have to be nice, okay?"

"The man in the ally?" Runner inquired, but no sound came from him.

The next day was school. Ophelia stuffed Runner into her backpack and she hurried to the car with her dad.

"Ophelia, do you remember my number in case you get hurt?"

"Uh-huh," She replied.

"Okay, just remember to be careful while you're at school. The teachers agreed to keep an eye out but if this public schooling doesn't work, your mami and I will see about home-schooling."

Ophelia didn't want to be home-schooled. She wanted to make friends with the other kids.

Classes were boring for Runner. Everything was dark in the backpack. He could hear voices, but couldn't make out the words. A bell rang suddenly, and it resonated within his whole body. It was so loud and disruptive, Runner felt disoriented. Ophelia took him out of the backpack and hurried over to a small group of other girls.

Ophelia stood away from them, hesitant. She wanted to make friends, but it was intimidating to watch the other kids grouped together. She held Runner close to her heart, took a deep breath, and forced herself to move forward. She thought of what her mami told her, 'You can't make friends if you don't try.' Ophelia stood before her peers.

"Do you like my new doll?" She asked them.

A young girl with brown hair jeered, "What an ugly thing! Where did you get it?"

"A man in the alley gave him to me," Ophelia told them.

"You got it from a hobo? Eww! You're so creepy," Another girl squealed. "Get away from us you creep!"

The girls rushed away. Ophelia's grip on Runner loosened a little bit before she pushed him against her chest even tighter. Ophelia wondered if the boys would be more interested in her toy. She went outside into the playground and looked for a group of kids that she felt she could meet. Maybe if she asked to be friends first.

"Hello," She came up to a few boys with a soccer ball. "My name is Ophelia, wanna be my friend?"

"What's that thing you have?" the boy asked, looking at Runner with disdain.

"His name is Runner," Ophelia replied proudly. "He's my best friend."

Ophelia felt her body jerk forward. A kid behind her jeered. "It's just a stupid toy."

Runner felt a familiar emotion. He felt it towards the boys even more than he did towards the stuffed dog.

"Don't push me please," Ophelia asked. "I can't get hurt."

"Oh really?" The first boy asked and pushed Ophelia back. "Why not?"

"Stop it," Ophelia screeched. "I'm really sick."

"Ewwww," Another boy cried out. "What do you have? Gross, I even touched her!"

"Why are your eyes pink, huh?" A boy mocked. "Your hair is a stupid color, too. Why would we be friends with you?"

"Papi says that red is a normal eye color, they're just lighter because I'm sick!" Ophelia felt hot tears forming in her eyes. "Why do you have to be so mean?"

"I saw your dad drop you off, you're the preacher's kid. My daddy told me you were dropped off and no one wanted you but the preacher felt bad and took you in."

"That's not true!" Ophelia cried. "Papi found me and then he and mami kept me because they love me."

One of the boys grabbed Runner's head and pulled him away from her.

When Runner found himself in someone else's hand, he got even angrier.

"Give him back, please!" Ophelia screamed. She looked around for an adult, but they were too far out in the field for anyone to see them.

"Or what, your dad will pray for us?" The boy with Runner in his fist asked. The boy started running towards the fence that separated the playground with the road. Ophelia, screaming and crying, tried to run after him, but the other two boys grabbed her.

Runner felt enraged. He felt more awake than ever.

"Don't! You'll make him mad," Ophelia wailed.

"Idiot, dolls can't feel anything," The boy clutching Runner's head proclaimed. He pulled Runner back, ready to throw him over the fence, but before he could swing his arm, he felt himself getting wrapped around. His arm was pulled back further. "Ow!" He screamed. He started to pant, trying to see what had his arm, but it was just pulled back further. "Ow, stop it stop it!" He shouted.

The other boys were dumbstruck, having let go of Ophelia, they watched as, for no reason, their friend's arm started twisting to an impossible angle.

"What's wrong," One shouted back.

The kid screamed as his arm went to its limit. It went further, followed by a 'Snap,' and the boy's arm fell loosely beside him. All three boys, screaming and crying, ran to a teacher. The boy's arm cradled in his other, twisted at the elbow, he only made it a little way before passing out.

When the kids were all interrogated, none of the boys knew what had happened. One said that it was Ophelia while another said it was the doll, but besides the feeling of being wrapped up and pulled apart, there was nothing the boys knew from that day. When Ophelia was interrogated, she held Runner close to her chest. "He was picking on me, and then Runner punished him," She said. "I'm sorry his arm is broken, but I told him to stop and he didn't."

Rumor spread across the elementary school. Some believed that Ophelia was a type of witch. Others believed her doll was a demon. Whatever the case, the little girl was never picked on ever again.

PRINCETON'S JOURNAL: CHURCH DOG

Dear Rory,

I'm sorry I can't come to see you and Sandra this holiday. I read that you needed to get Sandra glasses? How is she adjusting to them? I guess she inherited our family's poor eyesight. I hope this winter break you'll be able to help her cool off. I know she's so upset that I won't take her with me this winter that she's refused to talk to me for nearly a week. I figured she'd be upset, but with the events that happened over summer break I just didn't want to take the risk this year. We both know how much more dangerous these trips can be when the air is cold. We're still theorizing why spirits are more active in chiller months, and with the air being cold anyway it's hard to tell whether drafts of air are from the spirits or just a natural condition of the season. I'd prefer to know with more certainty how many dangers are around before I bring Sandra again. Besides, it's about time she got to spend a season with you. You both need a break. I hope your holiday is better than mine.

Actually, this case was quite harrowing. There was a lot to learn from animal spirits in this case. I've never heard about a malevolent animal spirit before, so I was taken by surprise when a pastor contacted me about an old cathedral that had this horrible haunting that involved a dog spirit. The church is nearly 900 years old, and it had withstood two bloody wars. It's a really famous monument here called the Fontain Cathedral.

The pastor, Reverend Noris Dupont, was kind enough to offer his own home for me to stay. He had a spare room so that's where I settled. It's a different feeling being in an actual home rather than a hotel. It felt cozier, the bed was soft with down pillows and a large, heavy quilt. It was perfect for the cold night, and he made me hot chocolate on the first day as we discussed the case in his living room.

He sipped his tea, hands unsteady despite the warmth of the fire. He had tired blue eyes and liver spots blotched all over his paper-thin skin. The reverend offered a smile before turning his gaze down to his lap. "I must admit, Mr. Figg," He muttered. "I have been a fan of you and your brother throughout your career. You have been documenting demons and spirits for seven years now, correct?"

"Thirteen, actually," I corrected him. "Rory and I just hadn't published a book about them until seven years ago, which spiked the popularity. But my brother and I have been exploring the afterlife realm since we were in college. He does the writing while I do the exploring."

"All on your own?" He asked.

"Well, most of the time. I sometimes have my daughter with me."

"You're a father," The Reverend mused. "I believe I read about that some years ago in an article."

"Reverend Dupont, I'm curious. Why would you be interested in mine and my brother's work? I mean, you're a Catholic pastor, and our research isn't exactly," I trailed off.

"You're concerned that your research contests our faith?" The pastor laughed. "I can see how you would think that. But that is not the case for me. You see demons as a manifestation of one's mind, collectively given power by the belief of others. You believe angels to be the same as demons, the same being given different names based on their malevolence. It is the same with religion. It is our belief that gives our God power over our lives. We put our faith in Him, and he will protect us."

"Interesting," I muttered. "On the other hand, I guess it's silly for me to just assume I know what you'd believe just because of what religion you practice. Making assumptions, I'm already making rookie mistakes," I sighed.

"It's quite alright, such things are bound to happen from time to time. But we are trailing a little off course. Mr. Figg, I asked you to come all the way here for a situation we are having with this dog."

I adjusted my posture on the couch and took a sip of hot chocolate. "Yes, when I heard about it, I was a little curious. I have never known an animal spirit to be malevolent."

"Did you not have a situation with a crow leading you to death?"

"That was only an omen. Animal spirits can be common signs that danger is near, though the crow itself was never a threat."

"Yes, well this dog was identified as only an omen at first as well. What I didn't tell you before, Mr. Figg, is that this dog has been wandering our halls for a long while. It has been a sight to expecting mothers or those soon-to-be pregnant for more than 80 years. It used to be very skittish, coming close only while the pregnant woman prayed. It used to be a welcome sight. However, lately the dog has been... Violent."

"A docile spirit becoming violent? That's impossible," I replied. "A spirit can't just change its direction. They're set on the same path. Demons, maybe. They can change and alter to match the unconscious will of the person it visits, but a spirit is always linear in its motive at the very least."

"Could it be possible that this dog may be a demon, then?" The pastor inquired.

"Even if it was, the motive wouldn't have changed so drastically, so quickly. At this point, 80 years of following the same pattern of being a comforting sight to pregnant women won't just change even in a matter of weeks. You mentioned this was something that happened immediately?"

The pastor nodded. "We have a pregnant woman that comes to the Cathedral regularly, she practically lives there. She came late one night to pray and she says the dog tried to attack her. It ran her out of the cathedral."

"She says that? Was anyone with her at the time?" I asked.

"No, but there have been other claims since then. Pregnant women are being attacked by this dog. One woman says that they lunged at her, she fell, and unfortunately the baby didn't make it."

I meditated on the information for a moment. I took a sip of my hot chocolate, thinking. "I would like to speak to the first woman that was attacked, as well as the woman who lost her child. Have only the pregnant woman been able to see the spirit?"

"Oh no, many people have seen it. It is only that pregnant women are the only ones who were able to get close and the only ones to be visited when they are alone. Some fathers claimed to have gotten close to it as well when they were with their wives."

It was a relief that I would be able to see what I was working with, but the fact that I would likely not be able to get close, that didn't help me at all. I sighed. "Well, I'll see what I can do."

"Bless you," The pastor replied.

The next day, I entered the Fontain Cathedral. Reverend Noris Dupont had his sermon and he urged me to attend. "The dog sometimes arrives down the hallway during prayer and watches from there. You're welcome to sit and see if it will arrive."

"I thought you said he attacks people now," I asked.

"Only at night prayer, when the women are alone. It seems to act normally during the day in crowds."

I sat and listened to the sermon. Out of respect, I stood when the crowd stood and repeated the mantras they would repeat. I may not be Catholic, but I've come into their house of prayer and I wasn't about to disrespect their practices by making them uncomfortable. I sat to the side, away from the seats, in a position where I could see the hallway towards the other rooms of the church just ahead. The other hallway was just behind me. I kept my eyes on the Eastern hallway since that's where the dog was mostly seen.

"Now let's bow our heads in prayer."

Every head bowed and many put their hands together. I became instantly alert, but I tilted my head down as well. I kept my eye on the hallway. Despite my best efforts, I could see no dog. After a few seconds, however, I started to feel uneasy, like there was something behind me. I turned my head towards the other hallway. I only caught a glimpse before I scared it. The dog was huge, I was sure the breed was a Great Dane. It shied away from me when it saw me looking and faded from view. I adjusted my glasses and turned my head forward again. I bowed my head and kept quiet the rest of the prayer.

Once the end of the sermon came, several people came to Reverend Dupont to ask for blessings and praise him for his good words. Everyone seemed so happy to speak to him, like he was a sort of rock star. I guess for the sake of the situation, he was more like a storytelling grandfather. You know, like grandpa Lyle who would always give us hard candy when our parents weren't looking. Reverend Dupont really had that sort of gentle, laid-back vibe, and I guess I wasn't the only one who thought so. Once everyone left, I came up to speak to the pastor. "That was a lovely sermon, Reverend Dupont."

"Thank you, Mr. Figg," He replied. "Were you given a chance to see the dog?"

"Yes, briefly. You never told me it was such a large dog."

"Well," The pastor laughed. "I don't think it would be so terrifying to everyone if it were a ferocious Pomeranian."

"I suppose you're right," I admitted. "It seems quite timid. It's hard to believe that a dog like that could possibly switch to being ferocious at night. Are you certain there aren't two dog spirits in the Cathedral?"

"Hmm, well I suppose that is possible," The pastor replied.

"Is there a story to the dog? Any rumor as to why it's spirit remains here for 80 years?"

"This is a cathedral with a rich history. There are three stories that ruminate about the Great Dane. One story is that the Great Dane is the dog in a story about how in the most recent battle, it belonged to the pastor who sheltered refugees from both sides of the fight who came in for mercy and healing. The church at the time was meant to be a neutral place, a place of sanctuary. The dog was left to guard the hiding refugees while the pastor went out to look for more people in need. When the pastor came back, his dog and all the refugees had been brutally murdered. The dog, they say, was pregnant at the time, hence why she would come as an omen to expecting mothers."

"That does make sense," I muttered.

The pastor continued on. "Another story is that the dog belonged to a nun who found a lost puppy and kept it here to have as a companion for herself and others, but then the nun and the dog died together from a horrible disease. The problem with this is that this happened over 400 years ago while the dog was around for only about 80 years. However, It's said the nun desperately wanted a child, but she gave her body to the Lord. It could be possible that the dog comes to mothers to make sure they're healthy, and she is an omen for a successful birth. Since the attacks, however, the most recent story," The pastor trailed off.

The pastor seemed hesitant to continue. It was clear to me by then that Dupont was fond of the dog spirit. He was at least fond of it enough to call for us instead of an exorcist like many others would.

"Sadly, there was a time most recently, about a hundred years ago, where there were rumors that a previous pastor had developed a sinful hobby."

I perked up a little. "Is that right?"

"He would find animals and torture them in the safety of his private room. As far as anyone knows, there was no reason rather than a horrible satisfaction for the pain of animals. The animal he was torturing when he got caught was a Great Dane. She was horribly disfigured and by the time she was found, she attacked and injured three men. They put her down. She was long gone by the time they got to her she was too dangerous. It doesn't help that that is the most recent tale of the three stories."

"What exactly did he do to the dog?" I asked.

"No one really knows," The pastor admitted. "It was before any of us were alive, and even those that told the story who were there never went into detail. The only thing we know is the dog was a Great Dane that was female and horribly disfigured. Although the timing of the spirit's appearance matches best with this story, there was no other connection between the violent beast and the spirit that timidly approaches pregnant women until recently."

"It must concern you that this story has emerged again as well, huh?"

The pastor looked at me with a weak smile. "I am worried that it will persuade others to leave the cathedral. A few of our followers have migrated to other churches since this story became widely known. I don't want this place of prayer to become a place of fear, and one child has died already."

"Speaking of which," I reminded. "You said that the woman agreed to speak with me?"

"Yes, of course," The pastor nodded. "She is waiting for us outside. She refuses to enter the cathedral anymore."

We walked out together towards a woman waiting for us in the grass. She wouldn't even care to greet us at the steps. I bounded my way over to her, offering the best smile I could. I offered her a hand. "Hello, my name is Princeton Figg. Thank you so much for agreeing to meet with me."

"My name is Francine Lachance, pleased to make your acquaintance. You wanted to ask me about the dog."

Her sudden business demeanor threw me off-guard. "Yes, just however much you wish to tell me. If you feel uncomfortable-,"

"It happened four months ago," She began. "I was in the cathedral, praying for a healthy baby boy. My husband at the time wanted a boy, and I wanted him to be happy with the child. Lot of good that did, next thing I knew I was face-to-face with the dog spirit. I remembered the stories that the other women had about it but I didn't think it was true until then. Startled, I stood up. Before, people would say it would run away once a pregnant woman stopped praying but instead it just stared at me with its cold eyes. I heard a growl. Suddenly, I was in a panic. I turned and ran, the dog chased me. I looked back to see how far the dog was and it was right on my heels. I lost footing and fell flat on my stomach, and then the dog spirit disappeared. My stomach hurt, I did all I could to keep my baby alive, but I miscarried a month later. My ex-husband believed I had a cursed womb and left me after that. My life was ruined because of this dog." She looked right at me. "Are you going to exorcise it?"

I flinched a little, involuntarily. "No, I do not exorcise spirits. I just try to keep the peace between them and the living, that's my goal."

"This is an evil spirit. It needs to be destroyed."

"Evil is not in the spirit, miss Lachance," I told her. "It is in the mind." I know this is a topic that hasn't been proven yet, but it was the only thing I could think of to say to justify not exorcising to a woman like miss Lachance.

"Are you saying that my mind is evil, Mr. Figg? I have lost a child and my husband and that is how you respond to me?"

"No, that isn't what I meant at all," I tried to explain.

"I agreed to see you out of hope that you would fix the situation, but I'm beginning to see that I was mistaken," She shot back.

"Francine," Reverend Dupont pleaded. "Let Mr. Figg speak. He is here to help, I called him myself."

Her anger curbed, but her glare towards me was as fierce as ever. I continued to try and calm her. "I'm sorry, Miss Lachance, I refuse to exorcise anything." I noted her jaw clench. "But I do promise to fix what I can. So please have a little faith in me."

"Faith," She scoffed.

"I'm sorry, you must understand what she is going through. She doesn't mean to be so cross with you." Miss Lachance clenched her jaw, but refused to speak. The pastor left to speak with some more people, and once he was out of earshot Miss Lachance turned to leave. "It must be nice to have Reverend Dupont on your side," She spat before walking to her car. I tried to understand what she meant by that. Didn't we all want the same thing in the end? There weren't any 'sides' in this situation, was there?

I spent the night thinking about my conversation with Francine Lachance. It was a brief meeting, she seemed to have her story almost rehearsed. She could have had to talk about it a lot to people wanting to know about the ghost and her child's unfortunate end. The whole conversation was tense, she was precise in her answers but also perhaps irritated.

The woman who first had the dog attack her didn't seem to want to talk to me. The pastor was doing what he could to convince her. He offered the three of us have coffee and lunch at a nearby café. He supposed a calming setting and a mutual friend present would help ease the woman's concern. She agreed, but even then, she was hesitant.

I planned to tour the cathedral alone and see if I could sense a room or area where there may be more clues. I had my equipment prepped, but since it was a place with many people, I couldn't use any cameras or recorders to avoid invading the privacy of others. This was a difficult case to crack. I first wanted to rule out the possibility of more than one dog.

I spent the entire day with an EMF meter wandering the Fontain Cathedral. I couldn't help but feel myself taken in by the gorgeous marble-work and the decorative tile placing. There were the usual many angels depicted as people with wings and flowing robes. The cathedral was enormous, I was sure I was going to get lost. I found myself wandering into an area that looked much older. I was worried that I might have found myself somewhere I wasn't supposed to, but the EMF meter picked up a drop-in temperature the further I went in. I felt a draft. It was possible the drop-in temperature could just be the weather, but I wanted to be thorough. I shivered, "This part of the cathedral must not have heating. It's so drafty around here."

Where before, there were nuns and some people wandering around, this area didn't have anyone. It seemed like the perfect area for a spirit to show itself. The tiling seemed much older, and there were more gruesome depictions of Catholicism in there. I came face to face with a statue of a creature. It was just a large circle of faces standing on a single chicken-like leg. It had small wings. I remembered seeing a picture of this angel before. I smirked at it, feeling more relaxed in front of this statue than I did any of the others. "Be not afraid, huh?" I muttered.

"You've come pretty far through the cathedral, haven't you?"

I spun around to the sound of a voice behind me. Standing there with a gentle smile was one of the nuns. "Yeah," I admitted. "I'm trying to find the dog spirit and figure out why it's been attacking women recently. Do you know anything about it?"

"Sadly, I do not," She replied.

My eyebrow raised and I adjusted my glasses. "Don't you nuns all live here? You must have seen the dog around."

"Oh, I have seen her many times," The nun replied. "But she wouldn't hurt anyone."

"The dog caused a woman to fall and lose her baby," I reminded her.

"Surely not our dog," The nun replied.

"Have you seen more than one dog around?" I asked.

"I assure you, there is only one dog here," The nun admitted.

"How could you know that?" I challenged.

The woman shrugged. "I have only seen one dog since I've been here."

I pondered what she said. "Well if there is only one dog, then it has to be the same dog attacking the people at night."

"Are you sure about that?" The nun asked.

"You said yourself there is no other dog," I sighed. "Who are you, anyway? You act like you know more about this case than you let on."

"I just know that the dog would never harm anyone," She clarified. "Are you sure that it's a dog chasing everyone?"

"Of course, it's the dog. All eye-witnesses say it's the dog." I looked back to the angel. "I mean, unless they're lying for some-," By the time I turned back around, the nun was gone again. I stood there, dumbfounded at first that she left so quickly. After a while, I started to think about what we spoke about. I found my way back as quickly as I could, and then I explained to the pastor that after I spoke with the other woman the next day, I wanted to come to the Cathedral after dark. The pastor obliged.

It seemed like a struggle to get the first woman to agree to see me. I was relieved when I learned that Reverend Dupont convinced her. The pastor introduced us. Her name was Diana Thomas. She convinced her husband to take care of their daughter for the afternoon that we were to spend together. Her husband seemed like the jealous type, since by what she said about the encounter, it sounded as though he was suspicious of me trying to seduce her. I assured her that was not my intention at all.

The pastor had tea and a sandwich while Mrs. Thomas and I had coffee. She was very tense at first, but after about 20 minutes of talking and sharing stories, she started to let her guard down.

"I have a daughter as well," I informed her. "Her name is

Sandra."

"That's a wonderful name," Mrs. Thomas replied. "How old is she?"

"She'll be turning twelve this January," I replied. "She's with her uncle right now."

"Oh, her uncle?" I could see the curiosity on her face.

"Yes, he's sort of my partner in crime. We're twin brothers, but he's more of a bookworm than I am. I'm more of a 'learn through experience' sort of person. We work really well together."

I could tell she wanted to ask about Sandra's mother. I'm glad she didn't.

The pastor looked over to me, and I took the hint to start turning the conversation to why I was here. "I heard your daughter's name is Nicole. It's a really nice name."

"Thank you," She smiled. "Nicholas was my grandfather's name and my husband and I agreed to name her Nicole after his passing."

"It must have been terrifying when you were pregnant with her to have this usually good omen spirit go after you."

Her smile faded a little. "Yes, it was terrifying."

"If you don't mind me asking, how did you manage to escape?"

I watched her eyes flash towards the pastor. "I just ran," She admitted. "Once I got past the front door, it stopped following me."

"Why do you think it targeted you first, after so long?"

She shrugged, looking off to the side. "I don't know, Mr. Figg. I'm only a woman who worships our Lord and wishes to do so in peace."

"You still go to the cathedral?" I inquired.

"Of course," She said. "I wouldn't let some creature stop me from praying. Every single day I've gone to that church since I was a little girl."

"But after such a traumatic experience," I pressed. "You wouldn't have wanted to face that dog again, would you?"

"Of course not, I," She looked at the pastor again. "I stopped going at night."

"I see." I closed my eyes for a moment to think. "I know this might be hard to re-live, but that night at the cathedral. What all do you remember?"

Mrs. Thomas looked down to her tea. "I was praying, the dog

was right next to me. I heard a growl, and as I turned to look at the ghost, I saw it stare at me menacingly. I got up quickly, but the dog didn't run off. I started to slowly leave, but the dog followed. I heard another growl, then next thing I knew, the dog was chasing me. Its teeth bared at me, I feared for me and my child's life. It barked at me, scared me so much. Once I got to the doors, the dog disappeared."

The pastor averted his gaze towards Diana, but he didn't say anything.

I remembered Lachance mentioning growling as well, but the barking was new. "The barking," I asked. "Did you see the dog's mouth move when you heard it? Do you know for sure it was the ghost?"

"Of course, it was the ghost, why wouldn't it be?"

"I only want to be thorough is all, Mrs. Thomas. So, the dog's mouth did move?"

She looked back over to the pastor again. "Yes, it opened its mouth and barked at me."

"Mrs. Thomas," I had to think carefully on how I was going to word this. I didn't want a repeat of Miss Lachance. "Animal spirits are not the same as human spirits. On rare occasions, you can hear a human spirit speak without tools. However, an animal spirit has no noise that can be heard by us."

"What are you trying to say?" Mrs. Thomas challenged.

"Animal spirits are not strong enough to emit sound. Their souls are too temporary, and too weak. They just don't have the energy stored within them to talk."

"You don't know that," Mrs. Thomas' voice raised. "It isn't like you've seen every single ghost in the world, Mr. Figg. And what else could it possibly be? I didn't lie if that's what you're insinuating."

"Well," I started. She stood up from her seat incredulously.

"I am not a liar, and how dare you try to take my horrible experience and claim that it's never happened! Women are terrified of this ghost and instead of stopping it from terrorizing the cathedral you dare claim instead that we're all faking it. Why don't you just exorcise it and get it over with?!"

"Like I told Miss Lachance, I am not in that sort of work. I'm here to keep the peace."

"Well the only way to make me peaceful is if that creature is out of the cathedral for good."

"Does it make you uncomfortable?" The pastor asked, surprised.

"Yes, it makes me uncomfortable, it makes ALL of us uncomfortable! It's always made us uncomfortable!"

There was a beat of silence. "Who is 'all of us?'" I asked.

Mrs. Thomas' face went red and she grabbed her purse before storming to her car.

"Wait, Miss Thomas," Reverend Dupont pleaded. She dared not turn around and left without another second's hesitation.

I watched her go, but didn't move to stop her. I sighed. "I get it, now."

The pastor looks to me. "What is it, Mr. Figg?"

"All the women that claimed the spirit attacked her. They all faked it."

"For what purpose?" The pastor inquired.

"From what I can gather, they knew you were a fan of my work. They wanted someone to get rid of the dog spirit and knew you would call for me but knew I wouldn't come if it wasn't causing a problem. They faked it all."

"But Miss Lachance," The pastor started before I interrupted.

"She likely fell over on her own, and a dog attack happened to be a better explanation. She used the dog as a way to explain her miscarriage after she fell over. She used it as a way to ease her own guilt. The other women likely fabricated stories about the dog in order to gain attention to themselves or they were also wanting me to rid the cathedral of the dog, or both things may be true." I downed the rest of my coffee. "They all respect you. They didn't want to tell you that the dog made them uneasy. Instead, they must have fabricated this story to give you a reason to want the dog to disappear. There never was any actual threat." I stood from my seat. "I'm sorry, Reverend Dupont. You brought me all the way here for nothing."

I could see the pastor's face fall. "I cannot believe all of the women would lie about something so important. Have I truly become someone they couldn't confide in?"

"They're not to blame entirely, and you're not to blame, either," I told him. "Hysteria makes people do things they wouldn't normally do. Not many people can tolerate the company of spirits. It really is quite rare for you to feel so easy-going knowing that an ethereal being just wanders your church. Don't worry about paying me, the ticket here and your hospitality was plenty. As it seems there was no issue to resolve, I won't ask you for anything more."

"Nonsense," The pastor replied. He sighed before he stood to meet my gaze. "I brought you here to settle the issue with the dog spirit, and you have done just that. Even though this was a mystery more than a supernatural endeavor, you still did your work beautifully. It was a pleasure to meet you, Mr. Figg."

"And to you as well, Reverend Dupont. May I request just one more night in your house before I leave for the airport?"

The pastor nodded, "Yes, certainly. You are welcome to my home whenever you need it. If your travels bring you here again, please keep in touch. Honestly, I would love to hear more about your adventures in the future."

Disheartened, the pastor and I went to his house. While I was packing, I realized that I forgot my EMF Meter at the cathedral. I took my rental car over to retrieve it.

The sun was setting at this point. I had to remember where I last had it. It was the spot near the oldest part of the cathedral. No one was in the hallways for me to ask for directions, it seemed as though everyone was in bed by sunset. "Wow curfew around here must be strict," I thought aloud.

The cathedral was illuminated with dim lights shaped like lanterns. The sun had set. I kept following the route I was sure I went to find the statue of the angel. The lanterns were replaced with authentic oil-burning torches. The older part of the cathedral was haunting, but it was also so beautiful. I was relieved to find the place with the monstrous angel statue moments later, and even more relieved to find my EMF Meter sitting before it. "There you are, my precious," I joked. When I got to it, as was expected, the batteries were dead. Well, at least I had it.

"I saw your other dog."

"WHOAH jeez oh my gosh," I turned quickly to see the same nun as before. I panted, putting my hand to my chest. "You scared the daylights out of me."

"That was not my intention," She replied.

"Yes, well, you did it anyway." I sighed. "So, what was that you said again?"

"The violent dog you mentioned before, I saw it."

"Oh," I relaxed. "Give it up, I know the whole thing was a lie."

"It may have been a lie at first, but I don't think it's a lie anymore," She responded before cutting herself off. She looked behind me, eyes wide.

I turned around, expecting her to just disappear again after I did. What I didn't expect to see was a large Great Dane, standing with its hair on end. The dog was growling.

"Wait, you're not supposed to be able to growl," I muttered. It responded by lunging my way. "Run," I shouted and ran with the nun out of the room and into the hallway. The dog followed us, it was too fast. "This way," I gestured. We rushed into a room and I slammed the door behind us. We took a few steps away from the door. "We lost it I think," I panted.

To my horror, the Great Dane phased through the door, still growling, and prepared to lunge at us once more.

"Hurry, over here!" The nun shouted, throwing a door open and running out. I followed suit, crying out for someone to come out and help.

"It's no use," The nun panted. "There's no one here anymore."

"What do you mean, 'no one's here?' This place was crawling with nuns and priests just a few hours ago!"

She gave me no response, just kept running. The dog was slowly gaining. I didn't think my lungs could take much more. We were in a part of the cathedral I never saw before, and I was just blindly following this nun, hoping she would know where we could go. All the while, I kept trying to rationalize it out loud.

"Animal spirits can't make noise, but this dog is growling. Can't be a real dog, it wouldn't be able to phase through a door. What made it so violent so quickly?"

"I told you," The nun replied. "It's not the same dog. Antoinette would never hurt anyone."

"Antoinette?" We turned a corner and I ran into a wall. I saw her crawling through a hole that was about knee-height. I crawled close behind her, panting and scrambling through as fast as I could. On the other side, there was a completely closed off empty room with shelves of food and other supplies. I looked around. "What is this?"

"The refugee hideout, don't you know your history?" The nun asked. "I found it one day and now I come here to read sometimes."

I saw something shift around in a far corner of the room. It was the Great Dane spirit, but she didn't seem too bothered by us at all. A little hesitant around us, but she didn't run away. Was this dog Antoinette? I heard growling behind me. Antoinette's ears perked and she stood up.

"Uh, quick, let's hide over here before it sees us!" I hissed. The nun and I hurried to cower in a dark corner. The Great Dane that was chasing us came through the tunnel and I prayed it wouldn't see us there.

Just as the nun said, there were two dogs. This second one was a bit larger, more menacing. It came from the crawl space and looked right at the nun and I. My heart sped up faster. It occurred to me. "The desire to rid the dog spirit, it convinced all the women to make others believe there was a violent Great Dane, and so here it is. They created a demon without even knowing it."

The demon lunged right toward us. I stood frozen, standing in front of the nun. However, before there was any contact, Antoinette lunged forward and intercepted the attack. Both Great Danes went after each other, biting necks and faces. I heard no noise from Antoinette, but the demon yelped and growled and barked like any dog.

"You can do it, girl," The nun shouted towards Antoinette. I looked over at the nun, her pale face glued to the fight, rooting for the dog spirit. My heart continued to race.

When I looked back at the fight, both creatures were fading in and out. They were using a lot of energy. I worried that Antoinette would waste all her energy and disappear. "Wait, don't make yourself disappear because of this guy."

She didn't listen, she just kept fighting. At last, with a lunge and a swipe, the demon dog yelped and faded away. Antoinette turned towards myself and the nun, her tail swaying lazily behind her. It was hard to tell if she was there most of the time. I wished there was something I could do.

"You did it," The nun cheered. She hurried over to the Great Dane.

"No, wait, you'll scare," I started. But by the time the nun got to the dog, the dog's tail was wagging more ferociously. She licked her chops as the nun embraced Antoinette. As she was embraced, Antoinette started to fade away less, but the nun no longer looked as solid as before. My eyes widened as the nun turned her attention my way. "Thank you," She mouthed the words. Everything started to turn dark.

My eyes opened. I felt like I was somewhere warm and soft. I moved around a little to catch the whiff of the quilt and pillow of the pastor's home. Did I dream everything? I opened my eyes and turned my body to see my EMF Meter sitting on the nightstand.

I walked out of the room to where the pastor was drinking some tea. He turned to look my way. "Oh good, you're awake."

"What happened?" I muttered.

"The night guard found you in a hallway, passed out. He drove you back here and I got you to bed with his help. I was worried something happened."

"Something did, I think," I told him.

I told him the entire story about how I met the nun before and what happened last night. The pastor seemed confused through part of it. Once I was finished, he said a few things.

"After you left, Mrs. Thomas called me to confess that she lied about the dog the first time. She asked me to forgive her, and I told her that I would, but you would have to know about it. She gave me permission to tell you."

"So I could be right, it could have been a demon."

"But I'm curious about this room with the lion-headed statue angel. We don't have any room like that, the whole cathedral was refurbished 300 years ago to what you see now. As for the secret room, that had been turned into the music room. The door to the music room was where you were found sleeping in front of."

"Is that so," I pondered. "What about the nun?"

"You never got her name?" The pastor asked.

"No, I didn't."

"Would you like me to find out for you?" He asked.

I took a moment to think. "Actually," I said. "I think I already know. It's alright, you don't have to go through the trouble."

Reverend Dupont promised to contact me if there was ever another issue with the Great Dane, which he was pleased to call Antoinette. Perhaps now that she had a name, the people in the cathedral will feel less anxious around her. As for the nun, I don't think she could have been a poltergeist. She seemed to transfer her energy to Antoinette, so I don't think she was a demon, either. Maybe she was a being which we've never encountered before. It'll be interesting to discuss the nun with you Rory. We haven't had a real discussion in a while.

He paid me and I was on my way to the airport. I'm writing this now on the flight. Brother, have you ever known any soul to interfere and save a life before? There had been lots of stories about that, hasn't there? They were called miracles. I've never seen an actual miracle until this day.

Since this whole talk about family, it made me remember how lucky I am. For everyone we've lost Rory, we still have each other. We both have Sandra, too, safe and sound. For this letter, I think I'll hand it to you in person. It's about time I came by for a visit.

With love, Your brother, Princeton

VAN RICKSON

My Angel has left me.

Here I lie, caged among the souls I've created out of malice and out of joy, trapped within my own mind, with my own children. There are nights where I feel so ill that I cannot bear the thought of waking, but still, like a sailor bound to the siren of the canvas, I am summoned to paint. Now that I have known the sun, I feel cold here among the darkness when before I found it cozy. My dear Angel. Why have you come to hate me? Why did you cast your halo of light to burn and singe me with such wrath? You named me Murderer. You threw flames at the only thing I loved almost as much as you. Have I driven you mad? Am I to blame?

I see your likeness in the prime, 'Fairest Lady Tempera,' frozen in time, the lady I dare not call Angel. I feared you back then, I worried that should I hold you, your light would scorch my cold hands, but instead I have made you brittle and turned you to ash. You gave me only warmth and brilliance. You had turned your diamond eyes toward me in awe of my passion and desire, but the last I saw them, your eyes had turned tired and cold. You could not say you didn't fear me. You said nothing when I asked. Only I can be to blame. You came to me in purity and I stamped out your fire. I caged you here with me among the darkness. My dearest wife, my lovely Angel. Now you are gone forever.

I awake to the scream of the doorbell. My bones ache, my body shivers, and yet I go to greet him. "Mr. Till. Thank you for seeing me again."

"Mr. Rickson," He called to me. His voice faltered. "I brought you food and medicine. Please take both."

"Yes," I said to him. The paper bag felt heavy in my hand. I set it to the side and pulled the door towards me. It stopped, and I look to the face of my friend.

"Van. I must say something or I may regret it my whole life. You must. Move on. It's been over a year and you've only made one piece. You're not eating, you're ill but refuse to see the doctor, I cannot bear to see a man I care for die."

I wish that I could say the sentiment had moved me, but whatever was left in my heart could no longer take any warmth. "I cannot simply move on, Mr. Till," I say to him. I see his plump body stiffen. "If I am to die, then let my soul be dispersed among my children and may what's left of me be buried with my love. If it is my lack in progress for my work that concerns you, I have another piece that will be finished shortly."

Mr. Till's eyes softened with a warmth that I have come to despise. "That is not what I am worried about, Van."

"I shall see you later. Please excuse me," I said and managed to close the door. I could hear him call out for me from beyond the oak and brass, but I did not listen. I left the bag alone to drag myself to my latest work. For the first time, I have devoted myself to a partner piece. After my dearest Angel was destroyed, the darkness became too much to bear. I had spent six months to finish the first partner, yet still I am cold. This piece, I prayed, would send me the warmth I feel I deserve.

My stomach demanded that I consume something, but I feared that I may not be able to keep it down. I had been drinking water, and when the hunger forces me, I ate bread. I feel like the birds my Angel and I would feed on our picnics. If I were I a bird, I would be a buzzard, licking clean the bones of what used to have life. I have given nothing to anyone. I have done nothing for anyone. If I should die, let the living keep me where I lay and forget me. I do not deserve to lay beside the Angel I have murdered.

I was at last given the opportunity to do some good. By no means, a solace of all that I have done, but perhaps at least something to leave behind. Mr. Till had come to visit again. "I have decided to leave a will," I told my friend. "Once I pass, my brother-in-law is to have half of my fortune. You, Mr. Till, can have the other half."

"You are not going to die," Mr. Till insisted. "You are going to be perfectly fine if you just eat and take your medicine. Van, please listen. I don't want your fortune. I just want my friend well again."

"As a request from a friend," I say. "Will you bring a lawyer to see me, so that I may write my will?"

Mr. Till clenched his fists and sighed, but nodded. I know that secretly he appreciated my final act of kindness. With the fortune that I have accumulated with his help in selling my paintings, he shall live handsomely and his children will inherit as well. As for my Brother-in-law, it is the least I can do for betraying his trust and not caring for his sister. Mr. Till made me soup and would not leave until I had eaten it. Our farewell, like every one recently, felt as though it were the last.

My legs can barely lift my feet. I dragged myself to the easel and canvas and picked up my brush. I have so few paintings left with me now, Mr. Till has done a fine job selling them. This house, however, has become empty. I have considered keeping my children with me for company, but I couldn't bear to further Mr. Till's worry with a sudden desire to hoard my work. Once the lawyer arrives, I shall decide where my children will be sent if they weren't all already sold by then. Besides, it was the joy of sharing my passion to others that made my wife so proud of me before. I could not, in good conscience, keep my art trapped here with me, except for one.

I keep 'Fairest Lady Tempera' with me over my bed. It is the only thing that urges me to climb up the stairs. I cannot sleep on the floor as I used to years before. The darkness is so lonely, and 'Fairest Lady Tempera' is all I have left to comfort me.

I look onto my current painting, the one with the brother. Her sensuality, her passion, I can only hope that it will consume me as it did when my Angel was with me. I wish for this piece to brighten the world as my wife had before. I wish for its partner to take notice of the flames and be aware of his cruelty. I want to be forgiven. I need forgiveness.

The Lawyer came in a few days after I summoned him from Mr. Till. I offered him a seat in the living room. He seemed to feel a bit of discomfort, but everyone did when they visited my house. I told him what I wanted. "I wish for all my assets to be split evenly between Mr. Till and Mr. Tempera. I will give my home and land to Mr. Till who I hope may do good with it. I give my painting 'Cold King' to Mr. Till and my newest unfinished piece, 'Vengeful Queen,' to Mr. Tempera. These partner pieces signify the duality of my passion and my curse. As my wife was my passion, it is only fitting to give my latest work to my wife's brother as gratitude for allowing me to have such joy in my life for a short while."

"I understand," The lawyer replies. "You also have a painting called 'Lady Tempera.' Will you be leaving that with the house?"

My head bowed. Truthfully, it was difficult to know what would become of 'Fairest Lady Tempera' after I passed. "My only wish for that painting," I decided. "Is that it is placed somewhere that it can experience great care. It is my happiness and my greatest joy frozen in time. It is all I have left of her and how things used to be. It must be given the tenderness of a child and the care of a priceless jewel."

The lawyer had me sign and then he left. I felt a weight roll off my shoulders. At the very least, I have left something behind to two good men. Though I am aware my brother-in-law feels contempt for me, I no longer hold the rage I used to toward him. He has the right to hate me. Though he is certain I had saved him from the creature that terrorized the town years before, I have never had the courage to tell him he was mistaken. With all his hate for me, I am not even worth the small amount of gratitude he does have. Mr. Till is too kind to tell me that I have led him to a dangerous situation as a manager. I do not provide content for him anymore, yet he still comes to me with sincere kindness. I know the frustration he has with me, and I am grateful for his patience.

He came to me again days after the lawyer arrived to bring me more food and medicine, as well as to take the last of my paintings to auction. I barely had the strength to keep awake for his visit. He ended up taking all of the paintings to his vehicle alone. He had me sitting in my dining room with a hot bowl of soup and a glass of water. "I am not leaving this house Van, not until you've eaten something more than bread."

Mr. Till stayed with me and spoke to me until my bowl was finished. He told me about how his three children and his wife were doing. He let me know about my brother-in-law who has since started arriving at the auctions. I ate and I listened, finding little energy to do much else. He told me to get plenty of sleep. "I will," I told him.

'Vengeful Queen' is almost finished now. I think I may have about one more day. I looked up to her, worshiped her, gave every stroke of my brush the passion of the violent red, the fierce yellow, and the magnificent blue that reflected in flames. 'Cold King' lay beside me against the wall, witnessing the birth of his bride. Her eyes were ablaze, her white dress scorched and grayed with smoke. She drowned in the passion, the last of my light. My hand shook but I forced it steady for the details. She looked down to me with the blaze in her eyes of rage while the king looked to her with the plea for mercy. He was a slave to her, as was I. My passions moved on to her. My life forfeit. With the final stroke of light, I put myself out and submitted to the cold silence I know I deserve.

ABOUT THE AUTHOR

The stories told in this book are inspired by the dreams and memories of the author. Jean has always loved to entertain and inspire people and hopes to continue to do so with the world they've created in which these stories take place. They tell these stories believing that everything can be a learning experience and that there is always a chance to learn something new.

www.ingramcontent.com/pod-product-compliance
Lightning Source LLC
Chambersburg PA
CBHW031128210626
46816CB00015B/1231